Daughter of Suqua

·· Diane Johnston Hamm ··

Albert Whitman & Company

Morton Grove, Illinois

Library of Congress Cataloging-in-Publication Data

Hamm, Diane Johnston.
Daughter of Suqua / Diane Johnston Hamm.
p. cm.

Summary: In the early 1900s, as change comes to the village on Puget Sound where she
lives, ten-year-old Ida Bowen worries about what is ahead for herself, her parents,
beloved Little Grandma, and other members of the Suquamish tribe.

ISBN 0-8075-1477-2
1. Suquamish Indians–Juvenile fiction. [1. Suquamish Indians–Fiction. 2. Indians of
North America–Washington (State)–Fiction. 3. Family life–Washington (State)–Fiction.
4. Washington (State)–Fiction.] I. Title.
PZ7.H1837Dau 1997
[Fic]–dc21   96-48129
CIP   AC

The design used throughout the book was provided by Peggy Ahvakana.
It was inspired by a pattern on baskets woven by Northwest Coast Indians.

The book design is by Lindaanne Donohoe.

Author's Note

The historical events upon which *Daughter of Suqua* is based took place in the early 1900s in Washington State. The characters themselves live only in imagination, except for Chief Seattle, for whom the city of Seattle is named. David Jennings is loosely based on a former Indian slave who lived at Old Man House Village, which is called Suqua in the story. The present-day town of Suquamish is one mile north of the old village.

Suqua comes from the Indian word *d'suq'wub,* which means "the place of clear salt water," while *Suquamish* means "the people of the place of clear salt water." Historically, *d'suq'wub* referred to the site along Agate Passage, across Puget Sound from Seattle, where area tribes gathered for centuries.

The canoe-maker story (page 29) has its origins in the Snohomish tribe of Washington State.

The talking-cedar-tree story (page 92) comes from Mrs. Lena Hillaire of the Suquamish of Washington, as recorded in *They Cast a Long Shadow — A History of the Nonwhite Races on Bainbridge Island* by the Minority History Committee of Bainbridge Island School District No. 303, Bainbridge Island, Washington, 1975.

Research for *Daughter of Suqua* was done at the National Archives in Seattle, at the University of Washington libraries, at the Suquamish Museum on the Port Madison Reservation, and at various other libraries and museums in the Puget Sound area.

Review of the manuscript by Suquamish tribal members Charles Sigo, curator of the Suquamish Museum, and Leonard Forsman, anthropologist, is much appreciated, as is assistance by member Peggy Ahvakana.

To those who carry on
· djh ·

Contents

Foreword

In the early 1900s, the time *Daughter of Suqua* takes place, the Suquamish people were in the midst of a transition from their ancient way of life to a new existence within the "modern" American society that was growing within their territory, in Washington State. Many continued to live in a small village on the Port Madison Reservation, at the site of their ancient home, the Old Man House, on Agate Passage. They were striving to blend their old ways of seasonal harvests of salmon and shellfish and communal life in winter longhouses with the new American economy, based on currency and wage work.

Although it had been several decades since Chief Seattle, the revered Suquamish leader, had passed away, the treaty he had signed with the United States in 1855, which established the Port Madison Reservation, had still not been honored. Disputes continued to arise over land rights and fishing rights. Nonetheless, the United States was growing impatient with the "progress" of the Suquamish and other Indian tribes. The government now began to apply its "Americanization" policy at the Port Madison Reservation. This policy featured the breakup of the village at Old Man House, the movement of Suquamish people to allotted lands, and the mandatory enrollment of Suquamish children at distant boarding schools.

Daughter of Suqua accurately portrays our history during this period. As an anthropologist, I was impressed by Diane Hamm's scholarly research, including her use of many original documents.

As a Suquamish Indian, the portrayal of the loss of our lands and damage to our culture renewed my anger at the federal government and its efforts to transform Indian families into "Americans." The insensitive policies established so long ago continue to affect the Suquamish people today.

I was very moved by the relationship between Ida and her grand-mother—the older woman still holding to her ancient ways, the grandchild facing a frightening new life and a great responsibility to survive it and preserve her heritage.

As a father, I was touched by the pain and courage with which Ida and her family faced their separation.

Finally, I was filled with joy and pride to be reminded that the Suquamish of 1900 were not a primitive people who needed to be "saved" from their own culture. Then, as now, we had deep love for our families, appreciation of the natural beauty of our land and water, and a strong sense of our community and culture.

It is my hope that this book will help to show that the Suquamish, as well as other Native American peoples, do not need to be changed or assimilated. Instead, we can be acknowledged as a race of people who have lived on this land for thousands of years and are willing to share it with others who will respect and honor our ways, our rights, and our beliefs.

Leonard Forsman,
Suquamish Tribe

Northwestern United States

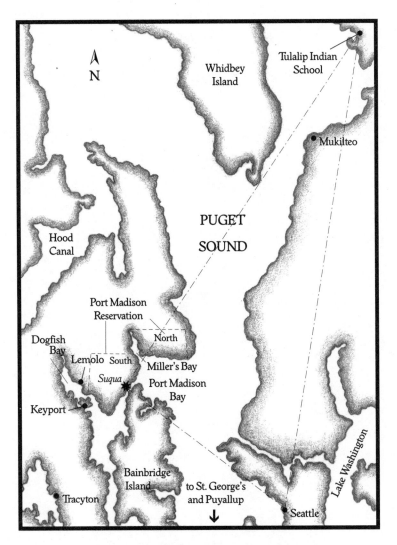

N

Whidbey
Island

Tulalip Indian
School

Mukilteo

PUGET

SOUND

Hood
Canal

Port Madison
Reservation

North

Dogfish
Bay

Lemolo   South

Miller's Bay

Suqua

Port Madison
Bay

Keyport

Lake Washington

Bainbridge
Island

to St. George's
and Puyallup

Tracyton

Seattle

↓

Area surrounding Suqua, about 1905

Daughter of Suqua

Chapter 1

Suqua

Ida Bowen's dark braids jiggled behind her as she hurried along the path, swinging her water baskets. Already, splashes of cold water had seeped through her dress. She hummed to herself to keep from calling out what she and Little Grandma were about to do.

On the slope above her, dark green fir trees rose into a cloudless dawn sky. Below her, the unpainted houses of Suqua slept on the beach like canoes pulled from the waters of Puget Sound. A seagull dipped and screeched over the sand.

Ida hurried past the mission church tucked into the trees like a small, snowy peak. She whisked by the cemetery where Father's first family, taken by diphtheria, lay buried. Nudging open the gate next door, she passed through the orchard and Little Grandma's garden to the house. She set the water baskets inside, her chores done.

Mother glanced at her approvingly from the double bed against the wall where she sat braiding her smooth black hair. Ida watched her twist the braid into a bun and fasten it with hairpins. She thought Mother the prettiest woman on Port Madison Reservation and hoped to grow up to be like her.

She wished Mother were a part of her and Grandma's plan. She hesitated a moment, then bounded across the floor to land with her knees on the bed.

"Whooo!" said Mother in surprise.

Ida wrapped her arms around Mother's waist and laid her head on Mother's shoulder. "Come with us!" she urged.

Mother gave her a pat on the cheek and got up to dress. Ida had known she would not come. Instead, she would paddle over to the island across from Suqua to do laundry at a boardinghouse, as she did every day but Sunday. Besides, Father would be arriving on Friday from lumber camp. Mother would want to be home then.

Ida sprang off the bed as Little Grandma came out of the back room, her black eyes bright with the same excitement Ida felt. Little Grandma was no taller than Ida but twice as big around. Her grey and black hair hung in braids to her waist. She handed Ida some quilts and a basket filled with potatoes, apples, and sandwiches.

Ida left the house right away with her load. She and Little Grandma seldom wasted words. When they did speak, it was always in Suquamish, the language of the People. Little Grandma did not speak English like the rest of the family, who used Suquamish at home but English at school and at work.

Ida followed the tree line instead of heading directly down the slope through the village where Teacher might see her. Teacher was also "Mr. Simpson," the agent for the reservation.

He was a paested—a white man—and made sure all the rules that were sent down from the superintendent of the Indian agency at Tulalip were followed. Ida knew he would not approve of her missing school today.

She slipped past Deaf Ellington's house and around David Jennings's yard where his tied-up dogs raised a clamor. David waved to her from inside his doorway where he sat at early breakfast.

David also wore his hair in braids, like the men of bygone days. Grandma remembered when he had been sold into the Tribe as a child fifty years before.

Ida waved back at him now. David already knew about their secret plan. He was letting Mother use his canoe while they were gone. Ida would have to give him a full account of the trip when she returned.

Just beyond David Jennings's house lay the beach where several canoes were pulled up on the sand. Beyond the canoes stood Teacher's house. It was larger than any of the others in Suqua, with four rooms and windows all around. Windows that Teacher or his wife might be looking out this very moment.

Ida crouched down and scurried across the sand grass. She set the basket in the smallest canoe and dumped the quilts in after it.

"Daybreak! Where are you going?" someone called.

Ida flattened herself in the grass. Tony! What was *he* doing up so early? Tony Canavaro was the only one besides Grandma who called Ida by her Suquamish name, which was something only a few of the old people still had.

Tony had been ten years old when Ida was born—her own age now—and had helped Mother strap her into her cradleboard. Several years later, when his widowed father moved off the reservation, he made himself a shack on the beach. His married sister, who also stayed behind, lived on the family place in the woods.

Ida crawled forward to see around the canoe and scanned the area near Tony's shack. Tony was nowhere to be seen. Smoke curled from the chimney of Teacher's house. To her relief, he had not come out.

"What a glorious day for a fishing trip!" Tony called. There he was—sitting on the floating dock in a dark coat and matching trousers and with a tall hat on his head. She motioned wildly for him to be quiet. He grinned and shrugged his shoulders as if he did not understand.

She was doubly annoyed at him now. Not only was he drawing attention to her, but being dressed in his city clothes meant only one thing: Tony was going drinking. He was waiting for the eight o'clock steamer to take him to Seattle where he could buy liquor.

As though he could read her mind, he called out, "What a glorious day to go to the city for shoes!"

She ducked back behind the canoe. She was not fooled. She wanted to run down the dock and push him into the Sound. Now she was going to have to spend all of her first fishing camp with Grandma worrying about him!

Tony always came back from the city with lumps and bruises and no money left for food. His usually teasing eyes would be cloudy as though he were no longer home behind them. His chin-length hair would be matted and his clothes rumpled as though he had slept in the street.

Mother had told him the city was not a safe place for a drinking Indian. Once, someone had broken his nose. It had a permanent bump on it now, not that this could make Ida like him any less.

Still, she frowned at him. As she crawled carefully into the canoe, all was silent except for the waters of the Sound lapping at the beach. She halfway expected Tony to sneak up on her. Instead, she heard Little Grandma approaching.

Little Grandma unrolled a cattail mat over Ida to hide her, then shoved the canoe into the water. Its bottom scraped against the broken shells of centuries' worth of Suqua clam feasts.

Little Grandma climbed into the canoe and used the paddle to push it deeper into the water. She seated herself on a mat and began to paddle, side to side.

"Good morning, Guk-kub," Ida heard a man very

close by say to Grandma. Teacher! Ida squeezed her eyes shut as though that could make her invisible under the mat.

"Good fishing, Grandmother!" That was Tony's voice speaking in Suquamish equally close by.

Peeking at Little Grandma, Ida saw her nod in greeting and paddle slowly on.

Chapter 2

Little Grandma

Grandma paddled evenly and surely as though leaving shore with Ida hidden in the bottom of the canoe were a regular part of her morning chores. Ida poked her head out from under the mat. Little Grandma smiled at her calmly, her face wrinkled as an old leather boot.

Little Grandma was the dearest thing to Ida on land or on water. She was Ida's only grandmother, and Ida was her only grandchild. Grandma had had three other children before Mother, but none of them had lived past babyhood.

Ida loved Mother and Father in a different way from Little Grandma. They were like her arms and legs. She could not imagine life without them. But Little Grandma understood Ida when others did not. She comforted her when Mother was too busy and Father far away.

It had been Little Grandma's idea to set up a fishing camp. Father had said last time he was home that with the coming changes even more of the old ways would be lost. "Both you and I went to fishing camp with our families," he told Grandma. "But my wife has never gone, and neither has my daughter. We will soon forget how to feed ourselves."

Little Grandma was not one to answer quickly, nor to speak long. She said simply, "I will take Daybreak to fishing camp."

Ida was so pleased she had grinned for days. Mother made sure she understood that this was the only time she would be allowed to miss school. Also, it would not be the kind of fishing camp where families gathered for several weeks. There would be only Ida and Grandma, and they would stay two or three days.

That was fine with Ida. Except for the time the whole family had gone to visit Cousin Magda in the South Sound, she had never been away from home before. Only if everyone came along could she imagine wanting to go anywhere for long. It would be enough for Little Grandma and her to be on their own for two or three days.

From Ida's hiding place in the canoe she saw her friend Katie Goldsmith's house on the edge of the reservation. She wished Katie were outside so she could wave to her.

Suqua and Teacher were far enough behind now that she could safely come out from under the mat. She rolled it up and brought out a paddle. While Grandma dipped on the right side of the canoe, Ida dipped on the left, pulling the paddle through the water like a spoon through a bowlful of chowder.

Little Grandma steered a course to the south along the shoreline of the wooded island that lay across from Suqua like a footprint in the Sound. In the underbrush of the island's always-green cedars and firs, the vine maple was turning scarlet and the berry bushes gold as though to warn of changing times.

Grandma pointed out a farm carved out of the woods high on a bluff. Father always said Grandma was the farmer in the family. She had learned about growing things when she lived among the Twana on the Skokomish River.

Ida gazed up at the two-story white farmhouse with its huge barn and mown meadow. She wondered how long it had taken to build the house and how long to cut down the trees and pull out all the stumps to make the meadow. She wondered if there were strong boys in the family to help and whether the father lived at home.

"When you are old like me, Daybreak," said Little Grandma, "maybe you will still paddle this canoe."

"Yes, Grandma," said Ida. She could not imagine herself ever being as old as Little Grandma, but she would like to have this canoe when she was.

Grandma's father had made it from a cedar tree for Grandma and her sister when they were girls. They used it to gather food and material for making baskets and mats. Now Mother used the canoe to get to her laundry work, and Ida and Grandma used it for fishing.

Ida loved being out on the water with Grandma. Overhead, the sky grew bluer with morning. A breeze began to stir at their backs, rippling the water so that it sparkled with light. She knew there were coho salmon under the surface, journeying from the sea back to the streams where they had hatched. She felt as though she were following them.

A while later Grandma steered the canoe into a tiny bay she had visited with other Suquamish in years past.

A swiftly flowing stream splashed out of the woods and down the bank. There were no signs of farm life nearby.

Ida stepped into the icy water and pushed the canoe up onto the beach. It felt good to stretch her legs. She and Grandma rested against a driftwood log and ate apple-butter sandwiches from home while their wet feet dried in the sun.

"Now we find branches for our house," said Grandma. She and Ida went into the woods and searched in the underbrush for branches that had broken off from the trees in windstorms.

In a sunny clearing Ida paused to pick the last of some late-blooming blackberries. For her efforts she got four overripe berries and scratches on her arms from the thorns. Grandma gathered several sturdy branches. Ida found mainly small ones.

"Little ones are for the fish," said Grandma.

Back on the beach, Grandma chose a flat spot above the tideline for a camp. Taking up a hatchet, she trimmed several of the branches into poles and sticks. Then she handed Ida a rock. "Now pound the poles into the ground," she said. "One pole for each corner of the house—a small house. And one in between the corners."

Ida happily did as she was told. When she was done, Grandma helped her tie crosspieces along the tops of the poles with lengths of rope. Then they unrolled the cattail mats Grandma had woven years before and tied those onto the pole frame to make walls. Another mat went across the top for a roof.

Ida stepped back. Before them stood a comfortable little shelter. "Just like Tony's house," she said proudly. "Except ours is better. We could live here all winter, Grandma."

"Too cold," said Little Grandma. She picked up several of the smaller branches and headed towards the stream. "You make the bed now," she said to Ida.

Ida pulled the remaining cedar boughs inside the shelter for a mattress. She thought about Tony as she worked. Sometimes he was like a brother, sometimes like a friend, and sometimes like an uncle. When she grew up, she thought she might marry him. First, though, he would have to stop drinking.

She hauled the quilts inside and spread them over the boughs. Then she joined Grandma at the stream. Grandma had already begun to build a fence of sticks spaced close together across the water. "A fish trap," she said. "The fish tries to swim through the sticks, but is too big and gets stuck. He cannot go backwards or forwards."

Ida pounded the rest of the sticks in while Grandma tied them together at the top. "A coho by supper; by morning, more," said Grandma.

Later, Ida gathered small sticks and driftwood for a fire while Grandma searched for large, smooth cooking stones. Grandma lit the fire and rolled the stones into it to heat. Ida tended the fire while Little Grandma returned to the stream bank to watch for their supper.

It was not long before Grandma plunged her hands into the water and came up with a wriggling salmon. She thumped it on a rock to kill it and, slitting it open, tossed its innards to a seagull on the beach.

She cut off the head, the tail, and the fins. Then she threaded the trimmed meat on a branched stick for Ida to pound into the ground near the fire to roast.

Next, Grandma took a pair of sticks and lifted some of the hot stones into a half-filled water basket. Right away the water began to boil. Little Grandma tossed in some potatoes from her garden. From time to time she added another hot stone.

Ida thought she had never been so hungry before and that roasting salmon had never smelled so good. Soon she and Little Grandma were enjoying the tender pink fish and crumbly white potatoes.

Ida continued to eat long after Little Grandma had finished. Everything tasted so good—twice as good as at home.

"It is many years since my last fishing camp," said Little Grandma. She rubbed her hands in the sand to clean them and leaned back against a log. "The fish are the same, but I am not!"

"People should still go to fishing camp," said Ida, licking her fingers. "They would like it."

"Some people do go," said Little Grandma. "But there are not as many fish now. The canneries take them."

"Maybe some people don't want to leave their work, either," said Ida. "Like Mother."

"Your mother works too hard."

"She needs to save money for a store," said Ida. "If Cousin Magda's house hadn't burned down, she would already have enough."

"A house is more important than a store," agreed Little Grandma.

Ida remembered how Mother had gone down to make arrangements with Teacher to send money to Uncle and his family as soon as she had heard the news. She had not even waited till Father's next visit home. Father had been proud of her when he returned.

"She does have enough for the cash register, though," Ida said now. "She told me." Mother had been planning to make a store in Suqua since Ida was seven. Sometimes they looked in the Sears-Roebuck catalog together to see what kinds of things Mother might want to stock.

Ida planned to be the person who rang up the purchases. She had watched how the clerk did it in the general store over on Dogfish Bay. Often in her mind she pressed the keys on the cash register and watched the numbers pop up in the little window on top. Then she turned the crank along the side, and the money drawer popped open—ping!

Most of all, though, she liked to imagine working alongside Mother. "Do you think Mother misses us?" she asked Grandma.

Grandma nodded her head. Ida moved closer and said, "I miss Mother."

Grandma put an arm around her, and they huddled

before the fire. After a long silence, Grandma said, "Once there was a canoe maker. He liked to work so much he hammered, he chipped, he pounded all day, all night."

"Like Mother," said Ida.

"Like your mother," said Grandma. "The leader of the sky people up above was angered. Too much noise. Much too much noise. He reached down through a hole in the sky, and he snatched up that canoe maker!" Grandma snatched at a twist of smoke from the fire, startling Ida into giggles.

When she had quieted, Grandma went on. "The people of the village wanted their canoe maker back. They shot arrows into the sky. See there?" Grandma pointed out a chain of stars overhead. "The people ran up those arrows into the sky and brought the canoe maker home."

"What did the leader of the sky people do about that?" asked Ida.

"He has done nothing," said Little Grandma. "The canoe maker is wiser now. He does not make so much noise. He goes to bed at dark. He does not start work till dawn." She gave Ida a squeeze and hoisted herself to her feet. "We do the same."

Chapter 3

Fishing Camp

First thing the next morning Ida ran over to check the fish trap. Shreds of fog hung in the trees around camp and on the other side of the water. Ida felt as though she and Grandma were the only two people in the world.

She got down on her hands and knees on the creek bank and peered into the tumbling stream in front of the trap. Five shadowy forms were lodged between the sticks. It had worked! The trap had worked. She raced back to tell Little Grandma.

"There are five fish, Grandma. Five!"

Little Grandma smiled. "After breakfast, we tend to them." She took up a flour-sack drying towel and went to bathe in the icy waters of the Sound as she did every day, all year around. Ida hurried into the woods to pee, squatting among the dried weeds that tickled her legs and bottom.

What if someone came through the woods right

now? she thought. Someone from a farm on the other side of the island? She jumped up and ran back to Little Grandma on the beach.

Little Grandma was already halfway into the water, undressing as she went. "My sister and I bathed always at fishing camp," she said, looking back at Ida with a twinkle in her eye.

"You did?" said Ida. She herself was used to bathing in a tub of hot water in the front room at home. She already knew how cold the Sound was. Even on the hottest days of summer, the children of Suqua did not linger in the water.

She made herself wade in up to her knees, scrunching up her face with the shock of the cold. Seeing Grandma already calmly sunk down to her shoulders, she pulled off her dress, threw it on the beach and quickly sat down.

In a flash she was back on her feet and running for the beach. Little Grandma chuckled and called her a wet hen. With her dress held against her, Ida hurried to the shelter to find something to dry off with.

That was one of the things that Ida liked best about Little Grandma. Even though she never made a fuss about things herself, she did not mind if Ida did. Mother, on the other hand, did not make a fuss and expected Ida not to make one, either.

The dip in the Sound made Ida feel as though she had mastered fishing camp. After a breakfast of apples and warmed-over potatoes, she confidently helped Grandma build a drying rack out of sticks to hang the fish meat on.

When it was ready, she and Grandma went to the stream and knelt on the bank. Grandma carefully pulled a slippery salmon from the trap, and Ida knocked it on the head with a piece of wood. As Grandma cleaned each of the first three fish, Ida hung the trimmed meat on the rack to dry in the sun.

Ida cleaned the last two fish herself. She took her time, digging her toes into the cool sand as she worked and glancing up each time a bird called. She liked this time of year with its leftover warmth of summer and its whisper of the mystery of winter to come.

She thought of her classmates as she tried to cut away the fin without taking too much fish. Wouldn't that boasting Leroy Halley be jealous when he heard she had been to fishing camp with Grandma! She was very glad to be away from the sound of his bossy voice.

Not that she didn't feel a little sorry for Leroy right now. Katie Goldsmith's mother had accused him of stealing Katie's baseball—the one her big brother who played on a mill team had sent her. Katie's mother was taking Leroy to Indian Court over it.

It was true Leroy had been the last batter to hit the ball on Monday before it disappeared. But Ida did not think he had taken it. She was very glad *she* was not being taken to court.

That afternoon Grandma had Ida cover the drying fish with a cedar bough to keep the seagulls from stealing it. Then she and Ida pushed the canoe into the water and paddled across the inlet to a marsh where cattails grew.

They pulled up cattail roots to roast like potatoes for supper. Grandma cut cattail stalks whose long leaves she would use for her winter basketwork and new matting. Ida arranged the roots and stalks in the canoe. As they worked, the wind began to stir, causing the canoe to rock gently in the water.

Ida thought of the canoe maker and his noise. She turned her face in the direction of Suqua and listened carefully. A new school and a new house for Teacher were being built up the hill behind the church. Every day for the past three weeks the sound of hammer blows had fallen on Suqua like hailstones.

Now she heard only the rustling of the cattail stalks. She thought of Leroy's taunting words, "You'll have to move as soon as the new school is finished. Everyone on the beach has to move, even the church."

Leroy's family did not live on the beach. They lived on land assigned to them further back on the reservation and would not have to move. "You don't know anything," she had said to him. He had given her a superior look and walked away.

Ida did not need Leroy to remind her that the Tribe's elders had agreed in the spring to turn the beach over to the U.S. War Department so a fort could be built there.

Families living on the beach would have to go to their separate land allotments scattered across the north and south reservations. No one but Teacher, who was getting a new house, welcomed the move.

Six months had passed now since the agreement had been made, and still no one had come to build the fort. Summer was over. Some of the Tribe had begun to believe they would not have to move, after all. Yet Teacher's preparations for leaving the old school were worrisome.

"Grandma," Ida said, swishing her hand in the water, "David Jennings says the War Department has probably changed its mind about building the fort, and if we're quiet about it, we can keep living on the beach."

Grandma placed another handful of stalks in the canoe. "We accepted the money to move," she said with finality.

A feeling of dread crept over Ida like the edge of a shadow. Little Grandma did not always tell her what she wanted to hear, but she could be counted on to tell things as they were. Moving to the family's allotment on the north reservation would put Ida forty-five minutes by water away from the new school and who-knew-how far from Katie, David Jennings, and Tony. However would she manage so far away?

Little Grandma gazed at her sympathetically. After a while she raised her head to the wind and said, "We sail back to camp."

Ready to abandon her worries, Ida sprang into action. If there was one thing she liked to do with Grandma more than anything else, it was to sail. While Grandma finished cutting stalks, Ida fit the sail pole into a block of wood in the canoe bottom. To keep it upright, she tied it against one of the canoe's crosspieces.

She laughed as she unwound the sail and watched it fill with wind. Made of stitched-together flour sacks, it said in all directions in faded letters, "Fisher Blend Flour." Ida's underwear said the same thing.

Little Grandma smiled. She was the only one who knew Ida's joke about the canoe hanging its underwear out to dry.

The canoe began to move forward as Grandma worked the sail with a piece of rope tied to one corner. Gaining speed, it skimmed over the water with so little effort Ida thought she and Little Grandma might just sail right up over fishing camp and into the sky. Into the sky where hammers and War Departments could not follow.

On their third afternoon at camp, Ida and Grandma harvested the last of the salmon and pulled up the trap. While they were cleaning the fish, two white men landed near the stream. Grandma went on with her work.

Ida stopped. What if these men took away their fish? What if they drove Grandma and her off? She and Grandma were not on the reservation. Since white men could not fish at Port Madison Reservation, maybe she and Grandma could not fish here.

"Do not be frightened," Grandma murmured. "The Treaty says we may fish where our People have always fished."

The men examined the stream and kicked away the sticks lying on the bank. Ida was very glad she and Grandma had already taken up the trap. The men returned to their rowboat and passed in front of the camp, paddling close to shore and staring all the while at Ida and Grandma.

Ida wondered if they were from the War Department.

After supper, Grandma sat by the fire and gazed across the inlet as though she were no longer with Ida at all. After a bit, Ida drew closer to the fire and tried not to think about Mother and Father. Finally she said to Grandma, "Maybe we can come to fishing camp again next year."

"Maybe," said Grandma.

"Maybe we can bring Mother and Father."

Little Grandma nodded.

Ida poked at the fire with a long stick. "Is this a good fishing camp, Grandma?"

Little Grandma looked at her fondly. "It is a good camp."

"But it's not like *your* fishing camps, is it?"

"No," admitted Little Grandma.

"Why isn't it?" persisted Ida.

Grandma set a piece of wood on the fire and settled back beside her. "There were more people then, more fish. Except for the last camp, the camp of my fifteenth summer. That one was not the same."

Ida rested her chin on her knees and waited patiently.

"Many people did not go to that last camp. Seattle, our much-esteemed leader, had just died. People were discouraged. Ten years we had lived on the reservation. They were not good years. We were often hungry, sick. Now, our leader was gone.

"I was glad to leave Old Man House—the big house on the beach where each family had its rooms. In my grandfather's time, great leaders from many tribes lived in the house. But no longer. Now good people and bad people, some from other tribes, took shelter there. The roof was falling down. I was glad to go to fishing camp."

As quietly as she could, Ida stretched out her legs and leaned back in the sand. Little Grandma glanced at her.

"But there were no stories at camp that year. There were not enough of us for games and laughing after supper. My father was silent."

Grandma herself fell silent for a while. At last she went on. "One evening, when night was lowering itself over camp, a Twana from the Skokomish Reservation drew up his canoe on the beach by our cooking fire." She motioned towards the beach and the fire as though she could picture them now.

"It had been a good day. The racks behind us were filled with drying fish. Father knew of the Twana. He offered him food. The Twana watched my sister and me as he ate. He had come for a wife."

Ida's skin prickled.

"He and Father spoke. As the moon rose, I was exchanged for three blankets. In the morning I went away with the Twana."

Ida shivered. "Weren't you scared to go with him, Grandma?"

Grandma seemed surprised by Ida's voice. After a

moment she said, "My father would not give me to a man who would mistreat me."

"But what about your family, your people?" said Ida. "Weren't you sad to leave them?" She imagined Little Grandma saying goodbye to her sister and her parents.

Grandma raised her chin bravely. "My family, my home," she said, "I took them with me wherever I went."

Ida waited respectfully for Grandma to go on, but Grandma had said all she was going to say. She separated the coals in the fire with a stick. Then, putting a hand on Ida's shoulder to help herself up, she went into the shelter to bed.

Ida rose and looked across the water where the light from a kerosene lamp lit the window of a lone farmhouse among the trees. She thought about how lonely Grandma must have been among strangers.

Maybe that was why she had come back to her own people. Neither Grandma nor Mother ever said how she came back, but Ida was very glad that she *had.* Otherwise, she might not have been her grandmother.

Ida went into the shelter and snuggled between the quilts with Little Grandma.

Chapter 4

Father's Visit

The next morning Ida and Little Grandma rose in the dark to take down the shelter and pack the canoe. They had to hurry in order to ride the receding tide home. Otherwise, it would be late afternoon before the tide would again be in their favor.

The air was cold and the water even colder as they pushed the canoe off the beach and into the Sound. Ida did not mind. She did not mind putting off breakfast until they got home, either.

They followed along the shore of the island that slept like an old dog on its stomach. The sky lightened before them, revealing the pale yellow grey of day across water and land.

Ida thrust her paddle deep into the water. Little Grandma and she could live by themselves with only what they had in the canoe, she thought. They would not need a house or land for a garden. They could eat out of the water and dig roots and pick berries to dry for winter. If they had to.

The closer they drew to home, the more anxious she became to arrive. She wanted to assure herself that Suqua and all she cared about in it were still there.

Katie Goldsmith's house gradually came into view. Her mother, Nellie, stood on the doorstep tossing out a pan of dirty water. Nellie's hair was uncombed, and she did not wave.

Ida supposed she had just awakened and was not in good humor yet. Maybe she and the children had been up during the night digging clams for her to sell in the city. Or maybe she was still cross with everyone over the baseball. Ida decided she had better not call out for Katie.

Soon the other houses of Suqua rose on the beach, with the church standing watch on the hillside. Smoke rose from the chimney of her own house.

Mother would be frying bacon, and the house would smell of coffee. Father would be sitting at the table pushing a forkload of pancake through a puddle of syrup on his plate. Ida strained to see if she could make out his canoe on the beach, but she and Grandma were still too far out.

No doubt Tony would still be sleeping. There was no smoke coming from his house. There was no sign of a fort being built, either. Ida relaxed inside. All was well. The War Department had not come in her absence and moved everyone.

As they paddled in towards shore, Father's canoe became clearly visible on the beach. Now she could see the gash in the side where Father had been tossed against a rock in a storm. "He's home, Grandma. He's home!" she called over her shoulder.

As soon as possible, she jumped out of the canoe and began to drag it up the beach. "You go on," Little Grandma said. "I will take the fish to David Jennings's smokehouse to finish drying."

Ida kissed Little Grandma on the cheek, then grabbed a bundle of cattails and an armload of mats and sprinted up the beach. She slowed down as she passed Teacher's house. He and his wife were at breakfast, she could see through the window.

She was struck with a desire for them to know that she had been to fishing camp—the girl who always behaved properly at school was rumpled and barefooted and smelling of fish: she had made camp! She did not stop, though.

She could see Father standing on the doorstep as though he had been watching the water for her and Little Grandma. She burst through the gate and ran towards him, tossing aside her load as he put out his arms and swung her up in the air as though she were four years old.

"We have fifteen fish, Father. Fifteen! And a basketful of cattail roots and — "

Father brought her back down to earth and cupped her face lovingly in his hands. He was several years older than Mother and had squint lines around his eyes from working outdoors. Ida thought his smile belonged just to her, though she was willing to share it with the rest of the family. "And what did you do with Grandmother?" he asked.

"She's leaving the fish with David Jennings." Ida put her arms around Father's waist and hugged him. He was not so tall as some men. But he was very strong from twenty years of pulling cross-saw in the woods. He was clever, and lucky, too, not to have injuries from so many years of logging.

Together they went inside where Ida hugged Mother, too. She seemed to be a little shorter than Ida remembered her. "A bath would be a good idea," Mother said, rubbing clean a spot on Ida's cheek. She dished her up a plate of pancakes.

Father pushed aside some papers on the table and, pulling up a chair, dedicated himself to hearing Ida's detailed account of camp. Father was only home from logging camp once a month and then for only two days. Always he rested first, then spent a long time catching up on the family's news.

Now, as Ida chattered on about sailing and cleaning fish and cooking over the fire, he said to Mother, "Any more children in the family, and I would have to grow more ears!"

As Ida spoke, she noticed the papers on the table. Some had sketches of houses on them. "What are these?" she asked, picking one up.

The paper showed a log house with a window on either side of the front door and a cedar shingle roof. Another sketch was of a smaller house made with boards that ran up and down like those of their own house.

"Is one of these for us?" she asked.

"One of them," said Father.

Ida was silent for a moment, almost afraid to ask what was on her mind. Mother would already have told Father about the new school going up since he had been gone. She would already have told him what Mr. Simpson was saying about having to leave the beach soon.

Father had not been home when the elders agreed to turn the beach over to the War Department, and he did not approve of their decision. But even he had said that the government gets what the government wants. Making an agreement had been only a formality.

Still, Ida hoped he would find a way for them not to have to move. He must! "Do we have to go to the allotment?" she blurted out.

"Sooner or later, we will move to the allotment," said Father. "I will talk with Mr. Simpson tomorrow to see what he knows. And here's your Grandma, what's left of her." He got to his feet as Little Grandma came in with only the top of her head showing above an armload of quilt, basket, and cattails.

Mother, too, hurried forward to help, but Little Grandma bustled on past to dump it all in the back bedroom. She returned to dish herself up some of Mother's hotcakes. At last she sat down, and Mother brought her a cup of coffee.

Father returned to his seat, smiling at her in admiration. He was very fond of Little Grandma.

Little Grandma nodded at him.

Ida held up the sketches in front of Grandma. "We're going to have a new house, Grandma," she said somberly.

"Later, Ida," said Father.

With her eyes, Mother directed Ida's attention to the water baskets by the door. Reluctantly Ida put her breakfast dishes in the dishpan on the stove and took up the baskets. Sometimes she delayed doing chores. But not when Father was home.

As she trudged down the path, she realized Father was expecting to move soon. Otherwise, why would he be drawing new houses before he even talked to Teacher? It was not a good sign.

Chapter 5

Mr. Simpson Says

The next morning Henry Roy, home from the Port Gamble mill, stopped by to speak with Father. Ida overheard them talk about asking permission to build houses on the land behind the new school.

"There's enough room for several families there," Father said. "We could keep the children close to school and still have a village."

Ida was so excited she could have hopped on one foot. All of Suqua could move up the hill with the school! It was not quite as good as living on the beach, but it was much better than everyone moving out to their separate allotments. She had known Father would think of something.

When he started down the hill to speak with Teacher that afternoon, Ida followed at a respectful distance. She knew better than to distract Father when he had serious business to tend to.

By the time Father passed the schoolhouse, Henry Roy and Deaf Ellington's old wife, Annie, had joined him. Ida could see Nellie Goldsmith hurrying up the beach to find out what was going on. When the group reached Teacher's house, only Father went inside.

Hoping to make the waiting time go faster, Ida went on to Tony's place. "Tony!" she called as she came around the back of his run-down shelter. In some places the matting was so brittle that it had broken off, making the walls look as though they had been gnawed on by Annie Ellington's sheep.

"Tony, we're back!" Ida always liked to give him warning, even though it meant he might hide behind the door and jump out at her when she pushed it aside.

Today, though, Tony was not waiting to surprise her. Inside, the one-room shack smelled like damp dog. A small opening cut in the wall threw light on a canvas cot with an army blanket and an old bearskin piled on top.

The only other furnishing was a rusting iron stove with a frying pan of dried-up beans on top of it. Tony had not been around for days. Ida checked the water basket by the door. It was one of Grandma's. Tony had worked two weeks in Grandma's garden in exchange for it.

There was still a finger's depth of water inside. No matter how Tony kept his house, at least he did not let Grandma's basket dry out. If he did, it would never hold water again without leaking.

Ida let the door mat fall shut, then pushed it open again to see if Tony's city clothes were hanging from a nail in the corner post. They were not. Tony was still in Seattle.

She heard the door close at Teacher's house. Father had come out and was moving off, followed by a band of people. Ida hurried over.

"What is it?" someone called out. "What did Mr. Simpson say?"

"He says you can't build on the new school grounds," Nellie hollered. "Can't you hear?!"

"Who can't build on the school grounds?" asked Annie Ellington.

Behind Ida, Simon Bonneville, one of her classmates, quietly declared, "We're staying where we are, on the beach."

Ida was confused. She pushed closer to Father, who held up his hand for silence. It took a few moments for people to acknowledge him and quiet down.

"Even though winter is coming," he began, "Mr. Simpson expects to see the army builders any day now. If we are still on the beach when they get here, we will be moved off at once so they can begin work on the fort.

"We will not be allowed to build on the new school grounds. Mr. Simpson says it is time, for our own good, for each family to go to its land. Those of us who have not yet lived on our allotments may lose them. They can be assigned to someone else."

Everyone remained silent for a moment. The threat of losing an allotment was serious, indeed. So was the fact that they might be moved off the beach with winter approaching. Even those who had already lived on their land were upset.

"But there's no stream on my land," declared Ellington.

"There's no beach on mine," wailed Nellie. "Are we supposed to eat pine cones in place of clams?"

"It's too far in winter for the children to walk to school from my allotment!" said someone else.

The problems of living on the allotments had been voiced before, in the years since the land was first assigned. There seemed to be no solutions then, and Father had none now. He went on home.

Ida felt as though a very heavy stone were sinking down inside her. With slow steps she crossed the beach and angled up the slope to carry the news to David Jennings.

David's pleasure at seeing her immediately turned to concern when he saw her face.

"The army builders are still coming. We have to move to our allotments right away," Ida told him.

David's face sagged with distress. "We should never have agreed to move," he said. "This is my home, here on the beach, among my people. My people since I was a boy."

Ida nodded. They were her people, too. She could see them disappearing into the woods. All the people, all the houses.

"First they did not want us to live in Old Man House," David said sorrowfully. "It stretched from here to Nellie Goldsmith's with rooms connected like necklace beads. It was the People's home.

"They burned it down. They made us live in a village of separate houses. Now they do not want us to live in a village of separate houses, either. We must live out of sight of one another, as though we were warring tribes."

Ida nodded again. There was nothing to say. They had signed the agreement. She turned and trudged sadly home.

Little Grandma was digging potatoes in the garden when Ida pushed open the gate. She looked up for a moment, and in that moment Ida knew that Little Grandma, too, felt as though a heavy stone were sinking inside her.

"It is the end of Suqua," Father was saying. He sat with his back against one of Grandma's apple trees while Mother gathered windfalls from the ground around him.

"Suqua has always been ours. A gathering place of our people from ancient times to these."

"If we were to wait patiently," said Mother, "the fort may still never be built."

Father shook his head. "Mr. Simpson expects to hear word any time now. That's why he's getting the school built as quickly as possible."

Mother put another armful of apples in the basket. She looked deeply disappointed. "The children will not come to school, scattered all over the reservation," she said, sounding as though she were thinking of something else altogether.

Father nodded tiredly and reached for Mother's hand.

Ida went quietly into the house. If going to the allotments was for their own good, like Teacher said, why was no one happy about it? Why did it feel like being put in the corner at school? In the corner you couldn't see anyone; your back was turned for shame. All of Suqua was being sent to corners.

Chapter 6

Back to School

It was suppertime and Father was still with the family. Usually, he would have been on his way back to logging camp by now. His extended visit confirmed the urgency of the situation at home.

"Three or four weeks I could expect the foreman to hold my job open for me," he said to Mother. "Eight years of working together counts for something. We could at least get a shelter up."

Ida had barely absorbed the idea that father might be home for a month when Nellie Goldsmith burst through the doorway. Panting from her climb up the slope, she shook her fist at Father and yelled, "If it weren't for you, everyone wouldn't be so stirred up and talking about moving!"

Mother invited her to sit down for coffee, but Nellie would have none of that!

"I am not moving. *Not moving.* They can build the fort

over me!" She thumped the table with her hand. "If it weren't for you and the others telling them they could have the beach—"

Father got up and walked out of the house. When Nellie realized he was not returning, she left in pursuit.

"But Father was at logging camp when they gave up the beach," said Ida. "It's *not* his fault."

"Of course not," said Mother. "Nellie just doesn't know how she's going to feed all those children on her allotment back in the woods."

"Teacher says we're expected to plant big gardens and sow crops for livestock."

"I expect Teacher has a good way to make forest into farmland, and fishermen and loggers into farmers, then."

"I don't think so," said Ida. None of the families she knew who already lived on their allotments had been able to clear more than an acre or two of land.

It wasn't so difficult to cut down the trees, Father said. The hard part was getting the stumps out. Most people, once they got a house up, went back to fishing or working at the mills or at the logging camps.

When Father came back in, he and Mother sat down at the table and studied the drawings and added up figures. "If it's to be a frame house with finished lumber, we'll have to sell trees from the allotment to pay for it," he said after a while. "To sell the trees I'd have to ask permission of Mr. Simpson."

Mother waited for him to go on. Ida carefully shifted position where she sat on the bed. As long as she didn't draw attention to herself, she might be allowed to stay up and listen.

Little Grandma rocked quietly by the stove.

"I don't like having to ask permission," Father said. "It's as though we were children."

Mother looked at the sketches again.

"There's also the problem of getting the trees to water to float them to the mill and then getting finished lumber up to the allotment," said Father. "It all takes time, and there's still the building to do."

Mother nodded.

"If it were a log house, we could use our own trees. I would cut them without asking Mr. Simpson. After all, I would not be selling them." Father looked up for Mother's opinion, adding, "Later I will finish off the inside for you."

Mother sighed a little. "Later," she agreed. Everyone

knew later might be a very long time away.

Nonetheless, Father appeared relieved. "I'll get Tony to go over with me tomorrow," he said. "We'll start cutting trees right away."

"Tony's not here," said Ida.

"No?" said Father. "Didn't I see him on the beach this afternoon?"

Ida shook her head. She felt ashamed for Tony. "He's gone to Seattle," she said.

Father swore in English. "How long has he been gone?"

Ida held up four fingers.

"He'll be useless." Father got up and paced the floor. "Henry Roy? Back to Port Gamble tonight.... Maldonado? More tongue than arm.... What about Bonneville's oldest boys?"

"School," said Mother. Ida did not want to contradict, but she knew it was very unlikely the oldest Bonnevilles would be in school. She supposed Father would get in trouble if he were to employ them, though.

"I'll go alone," said Father.

The next morning Father paddled to Dogfish Bay to send a message to logging camp. Ida forced her feet back into stockings and shoes and went down the hill to school.

She would have preferred to have gone with Father. But she was not about to complain when she could look forward to his being home every evening while he worked on the new house.

Not many children were at school that morning. Teacher frowned as he took the roll. Only four Bonnevilles, three Goldsmiths, Ida, Leroy, and Leroy's brother Donald responded.

"Where is everyone else?" Teacher demanded.

"Mathew and Rose are still in the South Sound picking hops," said Leroy.

"I know about the Miltons, Leroy," said Teacher with exasperation. "Where are the other Goldsmiths and Bonnevilles, the Roys…Greers…Hanovers…John Canton?"

"Sick," said Katie's little brother.

"Sick," agreed Simon Bonneville, though Ida had just heard him tell Leroy his brothers had gone duck hunting with their father.

"Our superintendent at Tulalip is also a doctor," said Teacher. "Maybe he needs to have a look at the sick students."

Each child present maintained a serious face, neither agreeing nor disagreeing that a doctor might be needed. Even the youngest Bonneville did not show any alarm that could give away her brothers.

Ida was tempted to cough as though she herself had been kept home by illness on Friday. Fortunately someone at that moment asked if they weren't going to say the "Pledge of 'legiance."

Everyone jumped up and chattered out the pledge before Teacher could properly begin it. "With liberty and justice for all ... for all ... for all," echoed around the room as each person finished at a different time.

Katie Goldsmith started singing "My Country, 'Tis of Thee."

Just as Ida and Simon joined in, a shuffling sound came from the back of the room, near the door. The other children twisted around to see. Teacher rapped for attention on the dictionary stand, but the children kept on staring.

There was little doubt in Ida's mind what the noise was. She had heard it before. Sure enough, Jethro, the reservation policeman, started up the side of the room with Tony, in handcuffs. The only way to the jail, a small room on the other side of the blackboard wall, was through the classroom.

The way Tony walked was enough to tell what he had been up to, but Ida could also smell from two rows away that he had been drinking. His clothes were rumpled, and one side of his face was swollen, with a cut over the eyebrow.

His grin, however, was unchanged. He raised his hands to Ida in greeting. She was so disgusted with him she turned away.

No one was left singing. Teacher sighed and motioned for them all to sit down. If there was one thing he did not like, it was having a prisoner in the school-house.

Sometimes a prisoner talked to himself or sang questionable songs. But mostly it meant someone had to bring the prisoner meals until the next session of Indian Court met. That would not be until Saturday. The someone bringing the meals would be Teacher or Teacher's wife.

For a moment Ida wondered if Tony purposely got himself arrested for drunkenness each time he came home so he could have a week of free food.

Teacher rapped on the dictionary stand again. "I have an announcement of interest to you from our superintendent," he said. Not until he walked down the aisle between the desks did he get everyone's attention. He clapped a hand on Leroy's shoulder to still him.

Once Teacher had passed by, Leroy popped up again and followed him down the aisle, imitating Tony's lurching walk. By the time Teacher wheeled around to see what the giggling in the room was about, Leroy had slipped back into his seat.

Teacher took a deep breath and returned swiftly to the dictionary stand where he began his announcement. "The superintendent wishes to inform us that the new dormitory at Tulalip Indian School will be finished at Christmastime, and school will reopen January twenty-second, on Treaty Day.

"As you know, last year there was not enough room to offer more than a few spaces to students from our reservation. Only the Tilmans went and Tom Flanders."

Teacher shook out the letter and read directly. "This year I am pleased to hold open fifteen places for students from Port Madison Reservation. I know many families will want to take advantage of the excellent education we are able to offer here, in addition to practical training in the trades and homemaking.

"Opportunities for the boys to play in the band and to participate in baseball, and for the girls to play basketball, along with well-chaperoned social activities, are other advantages to be obtained."

Teacher looked doubtfully over the classroom. "Who would like to go to Tulalip?"

Leroy's hand shot up like a fireworks rocket. "My brother and I will go!" he said. "I'll play a coronet in that band and first base on the team."

Teacher's left eyebrow went up, but he said nothing to discourage Leroy. Ida thought that was wise. School would be much more pleasant if Leroy went away. She eyed him critically.

His shaggy hair always looked as though it were trimmed with a hunting knife, and the rips in his trousers were never mended. But his appearance did not stop Leroy from giving orders while never taking them.

He made fun of Ida's reading every time she was called on even though he was reading a whole level below her. He'd find out soon enough who was boss at Tulalip, she guessed.

"Surely someone besides Leroy is interested in going?" said Teacher.

Ida shook her head. She was perfectly content to be going to the new school up the hill as soon as it was finished. The four Bonnevilles in front of her sat as silent as stones, hoping not to attract attention.

Katie slowly raised her hand after whispering with her little brother, who did not raise his. Ida was shocked. Katie go away? Why would she do that? And with *Leroy?*

She felt a twinge of hurt. What would she do at school without Katie? There were no other girls her age—just boys and little children. She was a year younger than Katie—did Katie want to be with older girls now?

"Three," said Teacher. He wrote the names down, then put the letter on his desk with a paperweight on top of it.

Chapter 7

Indian Court

B y midweek Father had determined it would be better if he camped out on the allotment for a few days at a time. He would get more done by not having to paddle home each evening.

Mother was worried about his working alone. "If you were clipped by a tree you might lie there hurt for days without our knowing something had happened to you," she said.

Ida was not happy, either. What good did it do for Father to be home from logging camp if she wasn't going to see him? It was all Tony's fault for getting drunk. Now he couldn't be there to help Father.

As she rounded the schoolhouse on her way home the next day, Tony called to her from the window of the jail. "Hey, Daybreak, how're you doing?"

"Well enough," said Ida, without looking at him.

"Ah, Daybreak, you're not still mad at me, are you?"

Ida turned around and scowled at him. "Father needed you. He only has three weeks left to build our house, and we don't even get to see him!"

Tony lowered his head. "Yeh, he told me he'd be needing help last time he was home. I'm really sorry."

Ida could see that he was. He always was genuinely sorry to disappoint people. But she was not ready to forgive him.

"I'll be out of here day after tomorrow," he said hopefully. "Tell your father I'll be ready to work as soon as Court is over."

"I filled your water basket for you," said Ida, and turned away before he could thank her.

Two Saturdays a month the Suquamish gathered at the schoolhouse for Indian Court. Fathers who worked away from the reservation tried to arrange their home-comings to coincide with it. Elders like Grandma, Deaf Ellington, Annie, and David Jennings almost never missed a session, feeling it their duty to be present.

Parents came with cases to be heard. Children crowded into the empty spaces and looked in through the windows. What went on at Court was often more lively than what they could make up in their play.

Ida and Little Grandma squeezed through the knot of people at the school door and found a place along the back wall. All the desk benches were filled. Leroy Halley and his family, dressed in their best clothes, sat in the last row.

Nellie Goldsmith and her five children, the girls in fresh dresses, spread out across the front row. Ida was still upset with Katie for volunteering to go to Tulalip. Nonetheless, she watched for Katie to turn around, to see if she was nervous.

It was Tony, instead, who turned and smiled from a seat off to one side. He looked as though he had been allowed to take a bath. Jethro, the Indian policeman, stood next to him.

From the back corner, Teacher, too, acknowledged Ida and Grandma. Teacher was a guest here. It was the Indian judges and the people of Suqua who were in charge.

Ida wished Mother and Father were there. When the whole family was able to come, she felt especially proud, as though they were doing all they could to help carry forward the important business of the People.

At the front of the room the two judges took their seats, and the talking died down. The first order of business dealt with a petition. Judge Emerson presented to the People a young man and his wife, with their baby, who were requesting permission to reside on the reservation.

The young man came forward to say he had long wished to reestablish his grandparents' ties with the Tribe. He had been to boarding school in Chemawa, Oregon, where he had learned the carpentry trade, and he now hoped to make a business of building furniture.

The classroom buzzed with commentary. One by one, the elders rose to speak. Annie Ellington mentioned the young man's grandmother, whom she had known. David Jennings spoke of the Tribe's desire to encourage young people to live on the reservation. Someone else mentioned the importance of training in the trades.

Each one extended a welcome, and the young people were encouraged to enroll in the Tribe. Judge Emerson asked Teacher to write the superintendent at Tulalip to see if an abandoned allotment could be reassigned to the newcomers.

The next order of business was Tony's arrest for drunkenness. He looked puzzled when his name was called, as though he had been so involved in the young people and their baby that he had forgotten his own reason for being in Court.

He stood to hear the charges. "Third incident of drunkenness in five months," said Judge Lawson. He asked for commentary from the People. There was murmuring, but no one spoke out.

Judge Lawson looked at Tony sternly. "Our young people are precious to us," he said. "We have high hopes for them. Can we stand aside and watch them destroy their futures with liquor?

"Many of us would trade our worn bodies for your sturdy young one, our tired spirits for your fresh gaiety. Do not rob us of the pleasure of watching you fulfill the promise of your youth.

"Think on this as you continue in jail a second week or labor on the new schoolhouse an equal amount of time."

Another week! thought Ida.

Tony's look of surprise at getting double his usual punishment turned to one of shame as he glanced at Ida and Little Grandma and lowered his head. He knew he had let them down.

The courtroom was silent for a moment. Then Nellie Goldsmith coughed and shifted expectantly.

"The next charge, theft of a baseball, is brought against Leroy Halley by Nellie Goldsmith," said Judge Emerson. Every schoolchild straightened up. Nellie rose to give her account of what had happened.

"That baseball come to Katie from her brother Harvey who plays on the mill team at Port Gamble. It's a real baseball. Been used in a professional game. Katie was good enough to let the children at school play with it at recess.

"That boy Leroy—" She turned and pointed Leroy out in the room. "That Leroy was up to bat and hit a pop-up—it was a pop-up, wasn't it Katie?" She turned to her daughter, who looked embarrassed.

"Anyway," Nellie went on impatiently, "when the ball come down, no one could find it. Not even me and all my children. That Leroy—" Nellie turned and pointed accusingly at Leroy again— "he put it in his pocket. My middle girl says she saw something round like a baseball in his pocket when he left for home."

"You were not there when Leroy hit the ball, Nellie?" interrupted Judge Emerson.

"I was not."

The judge did not look surprised. "Who was there?" he asked into the courtroom.

Ten children raised their hands. Four Goldsmiths, two Halleys, three Bonnevilles, and Ida.

"Ida Bowen, step forward," said the judge.

Ida moved nervously away from the wall. Her face warmed as everyone looked at her. She hoped she would know what to do. She hoped she would not make Nellie Goldsmith angry.

"Were you part of the game the day the ball disappeared?" the judge asked gently.

"Yes, sir," she said.

"What position?"

"Second base."

"And what position was Katie playing?"

Nellie waved her arm in the air. "Katie was playing pitcher."

The judge ignored her.

"Pitcher," said Ida.

"Does Katie always take that position?"

Ida cleared her throat and hesitated.

The adults in the room smiled to themselves, including Judge Emerson.

"Yes," said Ida. When it came to using her baseball, Katie was very bossy. She assigned all the positions, and *she* took pitcher.

The questioning continued. "When the ball was lost, was that the first time Leroy had been up to bat?"

"No, sir."

"Did Katie complain about the way he was hitting any of the times he was up to bat that day?"

"Not till after the ball was lost."

"I see. What was Leroy doing while the rest of you were looking for the ball?"

"He was looking, too."

"Are you certain?"

"I bumped heads with him looking in Ellington's canoe."

Nellie shouted out, "You see, he hid it in one of the canoes so he could come back for it later!"

Joe Halley, who had been fidgeting with the rim of his hat the whole time, jumped to his feet. "My boy is no thief! What would he want with a stolen baseball he couldn't even bring to school to play with?!"

"Maybe he was going to sell it to buy food!" said Nellie with a smug look.

Joe Halley looked as though he had been shot.

"Tssss!" The courtroom broke into shocked hissing. The judges' faces turned stern.

Last winter Joe Halley had been called into Court to answer charges that his children were going hungry. He had told the Court he had a lame leg and could not hunt. Living on his allotment a mile back into the reservation, he could not even dig clams. The Court had not excused him from providing for his family.

Several members of the Tribe and Teacher, too, had found odd jobs he could do for them in trade for provisions to see his family through the winter. Joe had performed each job.

The community recognized his efforts by disapproving now of Nellie's comment. This made Joe only slightly less angry. His eyebrows rode his forehead like hornets about to lift off. Leroy looked as though he wanted to escape before trouble started.

Ida stepped quickly back towards Grandma. At the same time, the men leaning against the walls straightened as though they might be called into sudden action. Judge Emerson ordered Nellie to step out of the courtroom.

Nellie crossed her arms and stuck out her lower lip. "I'm not leaving till I've got satisfaction!" she declared.

Both judges turned to the policeman, who looked suddenly ill.

"I need five men to help Policeman Jethro see Nellie Goldsmith out," said Judge Lawson.

Katie turned pale. The younger Goldsmiths slipped closer to her for protection. Eight men came forward, among them Tony, David Jennings, and Deaf Ellington, prodded by his wife.

Nellie Goldsmith sized them up. "I'll keep quiet," she offered. The men looked to Judge Lawson.

He held up his hand in agreement but ordered them to stand ready.

Ida glanced at Grandma, who had edged her closer to the doorway. Grandma's eyes were alert.

Judge Lawson continued his questioning. "Did any of you children see Leroy Halley place the ball in his pocket, in his cap, in one of the canoes, or in any other hiding place?"

All ten children, including the Goldsmiths and

Leroy, shook their heads.

"Leroy Halley!"

Leroy jumped to his feet.

"You are in the Court of your people. False testimony is punishable. Did you touch the missing ball after popping it up?"

"No sir."

"How do you explain its disappearance from the area around home plate?"

"I can't, sir. I didn't see it come down."

Judge Lawson conferred with Judge Emerson.

Ida kept her eyes on Katie, who looked tired and anxious. She knew the baseball was the only thing Katie had been able to call her own. With the many children Nellie had to provide for, everything else was shared, and nothing was extra.

"Loss of baseball is judged accidental," said Judge Emerson. "Nellie Goldsmith will pay the family of Leroy Halley one basket of clams to restore goodwill. Donations will be accepted after Court for the purchase of a new baseball for Katie, to be turned over to the school if the old one is found. Court is over."

Nellie looked out of steam and undecided about

whether or not the outcome was favorable. The children, however, sprang out of the courtroom like escaping mice and ran cheering down the beach. As Ida slipped out with Little Grandma, she saw Tony make the first donation to the baseball fund.

Chapter 8

The New Stove

Ida was sorely disappointed by Tony's sentence. Without his help, Father would continue to stay over at the allotment during the week. Certainly she expected Tony to never drink again after this.

She was also disappointed that Father had not made it back for Court. She feared he would not be back at all this week. As for Mother, she was supposed to have Saturday afternoons off. Recently, though, she had been kept late due to extra laundry at the boardinghouse.

Little Grandma said they would go ahead and make a kettle of Father's favorite clam chowder for supper. Ida helped her cut up potatoes and bake biscuits inside a covered pan on top of the stove.

She was setting the table when Father appeared without warning, tired but pleased at the prospect of supper with his family. Ida threw her arms around him and felt immediately more cheerful. She and Little Grandma set out hot water for him to wash up with and fresh coffee to revitalize him. Mother arrived from work soon afterwards and received the same treatment.

Ida wished it could be like this every day all year round—everybody home for supper. Father smiled as he sat down at the table and looked around at his family. As they ate, he told them about enlarging the little clearing by the creek on the allotment. "Taking down the trees will allow more sunlight for the crops," he said.

"Crops?" said Mother. Father always declared he was no farmer, never had been one, never would be.

"Of course," said Father, looking at Grandma with a mischievous twinkle in his eye. "We're counting on Guk-kub to make us genuine farmers with a big garden and an orchard."

Mother and Little Grandma smiled. Ida sighed. If only Father knew how much she wished that he *himself* would stay home and be a farmer.

After supper Father got out a Sears-Roebuck catalog Mother had gotten from the lady she worked for. "We will have a new stove for the new house," he said.

He and Mother looked at the catalog pictures and exclaimed over the features. "Two ovens, four burners, a tank for heating hot water," Father read aloud.

Mother smiled. Little Grandma shook her head in wonder. "My sister and I cooked on the ground," she said.

Ida felt vaguely unsettled by Father's taking an interest in catalog pictures—something he usually left to her and Mother. She glanced across the table at the upside-down picture of a stove. It looked like a large animal lying on its back with its legs sticking up. A dead animal.

It was not something she and Mother would want to sell in their store. "I'm sure it costs too much money," she said.

"It does cost a lot," said Father matter-of-factly.

"I don't like it," said Ida.

Father chuckled. "You won't have to wear it."

Ida moved away to sit by herself on the bed. They didn't need a new stove. She liked their old one with no oven just fine. It didn't take much wood, and it heated the whole house—the front room and the back one, too, if the door was left open between them.

And she liked their old house, too. She liked the

clothes pegs on the wall and the flowered curtains at the windows. She liked the shelves along the back wall filled with jars of Mother's canned fruit and baskets of Grandma's dried fruit.

She studied her parents. They seemed excited as children. They didn't even seem to mind moving away from Suqua now—Suqua that wasn't going to be there anymore.

"What about Indian Court?" she asked suddenly.

Mother and Father both looked up. "Yes?" said Father.

Ida could not believe they had not thought about Indian Court. What would happen to Court when they all moved away?

"We will come back for it," said Little Grandma from her rocking chair by the stove. Father and Mother returned to their catalog order. Ida went over and sat in Little Grandma's lap, something she had not done since she was six.

A troubling thought about the stove occurred to Ida in the night. It still worried her the next morning when she went out with Father to the three-sided woodshed to split a supply of firewood for Mother.

It was Ida's job to help Father sharpen the ax. She was

the one to turn the huge stone grinding wheel in its wooden stand so that Father could press the ax head against it to make a good cutting edge.

Sometimes she liked to go out and turn the grinding wheel when Father was away at lumber camp. It gave her a feeling that he was close by. She also imagined that it helped to bring him home.

Usually when Father was home, she did not worry about anything. But that was not so now. As they approached the grinding wheel, she blurted out, "How can Mother have a new stove, Father? We need to save the money for her store!"

Father stopped and looked at her thoughtfully. "There isn't going to be a store, Ida," he said quietly. "Not now that we are all leaving the beach." He took up his ax and examined the blade.

Ida squeezed her eyes shut to keep from crying. It was exactly as she had feared. Without Suqua, there could be no store. She and Mother would not be looking at catalog pictures anymore. They were not going to work together behind the counter, Mother getting things out for customers and Ida operating the cash register.

"Where's my wheel turner?" Father said. Ida dashed

away the tears in the corners of her eyes and took hold of the handle that stuck out from the heavy wheel. The more she cranked it, the faster the wheel went around, finally taking on a life of its own.

When she had brought it back to the proper speed, Father pressed the ax blade against it. Little sparks flew out as the wheel scraped against the metal. After a minute, Father pulled the ax back and checked the blade. Then he straightened up and looked across Grandma's orchard of apple, plum, and pear trees.

"Leaving Suqua is hard for all of us, Daughter," he said. "If you could look into our hearts, you would see that they wail like orphaned children. But wailing won't save us. If we don't make some happiness in the midst of our difficulties, we won't survive."

He put the blade to the stone again, pulled it away, and set it at a different angle.

Chapter 9

Lullaby for Suqua

The next morning, before Father left for the allotment, he took apart the grinding wheel and its stand and carried them in two separate loads to the canoe. He said that now he had a greater need of a sharp ax on the allotment than at home.

Seeing Father lower the wheel into the canoe, Ida felt unneeded, like the little two-lidded stove that would not be making the move. She understood now that the new stove was Father's way of trying to make a little happiness for Mother, but it did not make *her* feel any better.

Mother had not spoken of the store, and Ida did not expect that she would. Not Mother, who did not fuss over things that could not be helped. Ida felt a flicker of pride in her, but mostly she felt lonely. Everything seemed to be drifting away—Suqua, Katie, the store.

She watched forlornly as Father paddled off.

A chilly breeze had roughened the waters of the Sound. Overhead, a flock of honking geese merged into formation. October had come. She turned away from the beach and trudged on to school.

Tony had decided, as she knew he would, to work on the new school instead of staying in jail. Every day he stopped by the house on his way to work and again on his way home. Once he stayed for dinner.

Ida still did not feel friendly towards him. She could not forget that he could have been helping Father if it were not for the drinking, and that Father could then have been home at night.

Sensing her unhappiness, Tony did not tease her.

On Friday, at midday recess when Teacher was up the hill inspecting the new school, Mathew and little Rose Milton arrived back from picking hops in the South Sound. Rose, who spoke only the little bit of English she had learned from occasional visits to school the year before, wanted Ida to see her new dress.

"Did you get it in Seattle?" Ida asked encouragingly.

Rose nodded and hid herself behind her brother.

Mathew tried to shake her free. "Stop it, Rose," he said. He straightened his new coat. Then, with great importance, he pulled from one of its pockets a note folded into a star shape. "From your cousin," he said, presenting it to Ida.

"Magda!" Ida exclaimed. "You saw her in Puyallup!"

Mathew nodded, trying not to look too pleased at Ida's enthusiasm.

Ida carefully opened the star. "Cousin Ida," it said inside, "I wish you were in the hop fields with us. Come to school at St. George's this year! —Magda."

Ida grinned for the first time all week. Her cousin's letters were always the same. Come to St. George's. Come to the hop fields. Ida wished she saw her perky cousin more than once every other year or so. She looked down at Mathew. "Did Magda say anything else?"

Mathew shook his head and went off with Rose still attached.

Ida had just read over the note again when Katie exclaimed behind her, "St. George's! Are you going to St. George's boarding school?"

Ida dashed the note away. She had no intention of going to St. George's, but she did not want Katie to know that. Katie, after all, was deserting her to go to Tulalip. "Maybe," she said.

"Oh," said Katie, her face falling. "I'll be the only girl my age left at school."

"There'll be lots of girls at Tulalip."

"Mother says I can't go to Tulalip. Absolutely not. People die there."

"They do?" said Ida.

"Remember Sadie Nichols—George Tilman's cousin from Mukilteo? She's the one that died. Pneumonia. People die at boarding school all the time."

"Nobody dies at St. George's," Ida said without certainty. "My cousin would have told me." She refolded the note and put it into her dress pocket.

"Do stay at school here," pleaded Katie, linking her arm in Ida's. "Then we can still be together."

Ida held back a moment. But she was so relieved at being able to count on Katie again, that she blurted out, "All right. I will!" The two of them went off to play a game of post office with the little girls.

Without Katie's ball there were no midday baseball games for the boys and older girls. To make up for it, Leroy organized all the boys into a marching company.

"Like at Tulalip," he said. "You have to march everyplace you go there."

He placed Mathew in his new coat at the head of the company and marched them through the girls' post office game, out the schoolyard, down the beach, and into the water. Two of the three Bonnevilles refused to go in, and a scuffle broke out.

The girls raced down the beach to see what was going on. Soon half the children were either sandy or wet. Ida wished Teacher would get back from the new school site.

In the middle of the free-for-all, Tony and David Jennings were spotted paddling towards the beach in David's frayed canoe. The boys ran off to greet them.

Ida wondered why Tony was not up working on the school. She suspected him of playing hooky. Maybe Teacher was late because he was looking for Tony. She and Katie wandered down the beach where the boys were helping unload a large seal David and Tony had speared.

"Feast tonight, feast tonight!" Leroy hollered as he helped drag the carcass up the beach. All the children but the Miltons, who lived on the north reservation, and Ida and Katie, immediately scattered for home to announce the feast before Teacher could get back.

David Jennings and Tony beamed with pride. Tony began to carve up the seal. "We passed by the north reservation to invite everyone there," he said to Ida.

"Father, too?" she asked.

"Of course!" said Tony. "And your family, too, Rose."

Ida was so pleased Father would be present that she could have given Tony a kiss, but he was looking very messy from his gutting work. Gathering to eat together on the beach was one of Ida's favorite occasions. She felt as though she were surrounded by aunts and uncles and cousins. She, too, rushed home to tell the news.

Teacher at last returned and after being informed of the feast, much belatedly rang the bell for the afternoon session. Ida noticed that he turned his back to the beach as though to avoid spoiling things by finding Tony at work there. Inside the classroom everyone squirmed with anticipation, including Ida. Finally Teacher gave up and dismissed school early.

Ida took little Rose with her since Rose's father had not come to row her and Mathew home. "He's coming later for the feast," Ida reassured her in Suquamish. "Tony said he is. Your father would not forget you."

Rose helped Ida and Little Grandma dig the last of the potatoes from Grandma's garden to take to the feast. Grandma also took some cattail roots from her root cellar in the hillside for the older people who especially liked old-time food.

Ida and Rose helped haul the roots and potatoes to the beach in baskets. At the fire pit, Tony and David Jennings had so many children helping they could hardly maneuver the hot stones around the seaweed-wrapped meat. Women were burying bread in the ashes to bake. Grandma put stones of her own in the fire to heat for cooking.

When the children spotted Ida's mother returning from work, they raced to the water to tell her she was the honored guest at the feast. It was just for her. When she looked very much puzzled, they burst out laughing and ran off.

Father arrived, and the Miltons, and Carl Bonneville. Each was greeted with the same story, till everyone felt, if not the honored guest, at least very much welcome at the festivities.

In the middle of all the activity, Annie Ellington stepped on something round and hard in the sand. She reached down and scooped up the lost baseball.

Within moments she was surrounded by whooping, cheering children. Nellie Goldsmith at first looked baffled, then sheepish. In the end, she grinned from one side of her face to the other.

Annie entrusted the ball to a jubilant Katie, and Leroy's little brother ran off for the broken canoe paddle that served as a bat. A game was organized.

The men declared themselves one team; the boys and older girls formed the other. David Jennings appointed himself umpire, and Nellie Goldsmith hurried over to supervise first base.

Around the fire pit, Tony suddenly found himself alone with the cooking food. Mother and Little Grandma laughed.

"Go join the game," Mother urged him. "We'll keep watch on supper."

Tony wiped his hands on his clothes and hurried off to cover second base.

Ida and Katie ended up last in the batting line-up. But Ida was so pleased to have Father pitching and Tony waving at her from second that she did not care if she got a chance to hit or not.

Simon was first up. He whacked the ball to left field and raced off while Teacher leapt forward to keep the ball from rolling into the Sound.

Snatching the ball up, Teacher launched it at Tony who, unbelievably, dropped it at second, while Simon raced on to third base.

"Stay! Stay!" screamed the girls.

"Run! Run!" hollered the boys.

Tony sent the recovered ball screaming past the pitcher to Simon's father at home plate. Simon stayed.

Leroy stepped up to the plate next. Ida's father delivered the pitch. Leroy swung and missed. "Strike one!" called David Jennings.

"Booo!" yelled the children.

On the second pitch Leroy swung so hard he spun himself around. The ball popped straight up in the air and came down with a splat in Grandma's basket of cooking cattail roots.

Amidst much laughter, Grandma fished the ball out with a pair of sticks, and the women called everyone to supper. The children scrambled for plates and tried to hurry the grownups along, since it would be disrespectful to rush ahead of them.

Dusk slipped across the sky as neighbors and friends clustered in shifting groups to comment on the fishing, the availability of work, the coming winter. The forced move from Suqua was mentioned here and there, but no one wanted to talk much about such a worrisome thing. No one wished to give it power over the occasion.

The chill of evening drew everyone closer to the fire. The children stuffed down a final serving of bread and meat and nestled back into their families. David Jennings began to tell the story of the speaking cedar tree.

"Rain comes down like a river from the sky. It sweeps away the dirt from the roots of the giant cedar." David moved his hands like the river of rain. "Wind hits against the tree like a blanket being shaken by a wild woman. The tree begins to lose its hold. It begins to fall."

The children around the fire leaned forward as though they, too, were falling.

"'Help! Help!' the tree calls out to your grandfathers who are coming down the river. 'If you cover my roots so that I will not fall over now, in many years, when I can no longer stand, you can make me into a canoe, and I will carry you and your families to paradise.'"

Ida had never known her own grandfathers. She imagined, instead, David Jennings at the foot of the cedar tree. David, too, seemed to see himself there as he went on. "We cover the roots, and the tree stands many years more. One day when we come again to that place, we find the tree on its side. We carve it into a giant canoe and load our families and all our belongings into it."

Everyone present imagined themselves there, loading their belongings into the canoe.

"The canoe carries us here, to Suqua, our home that we cherish. We know no paradise but this." David leaned back, his story finished.

"It is true," murmured someone.

"Our people have started over before just as we must start over now," someone else pointed out.

Families began to drift quietly home in the dark, Deaf Ellington guiding Annie, who did not see so well at night, Tony carrying the sleepy Mathew to his family's canoe, and Ida walking beside Father, her hand in his.

Mother followed behind with Little Grandma who chanted a lullaby, a lullaby for Suqua.

Chapter 10

The Web of Life

O ctober was passing. Tony had worked off his punishment and was now with Father. One more week, though, and Father must return to logging camp, whether the house was finished or not. To Ida's dismay, he and Tony had not been back from the allotment for many days.

On Saturday she longed to paddle over to the north reservation with Little Grandma, but Mother had taken the canoe to work. Maybe they could go on Sunday, said Little Grandma.

That evening as Ida dried the dishes, Tony turned up at the house alone. Mother clutched at her collar. "What has happened?" she demanded. Ida knew Tony would not look so calm if something terrible had occurred, but she did wonder if he had quit working. Little Grandma began to warm him some supper.

"Everything is fine," Tony reassured them. "I'm just here for supplies. I'm to paddle you over to the farm tomorrow if you'd like to go."

Ida was so pleased that Father had sent for them she threw her arms around Tony's neck from behind, nearly choking him. Mother, who had been in a quiet mood, smiled and swept around the table, setting out canned fruit and beans, bread, and rice to take to Father.

The next morning was misty and cold. Mother wanted Ida to put on her stockings and shoes.

"They'll just get wet in the grass," Ida said. Stockings that came clear to the tops of her legs were a nuisance any-time, but could hardly be expected to stay up on a march through the brush.

Instead, she put on her winter coat and left her feet bare like Grandma's. Tony hurried the loading of the canoe, as the tide would soon be turning.

Mother, Ida, and Little Grandma quickly settled themselves among the bundles of food and garden tools. Tony shoved the canoe into the Sound and took up a paddle. The rest of the village slept, fog easing between the rooftops.

As the canoe pressed forward like a sea otter, the land

of the south reservation curved off to the left, dimpling into tiny Miller's Bay. Tony said that was where he and David Jennings had gotten the seal.

As they crossed larger Port Madison Bay, bits of sunlight filtered down through the mist. Ida imagined herself in the talking cedar canoe on the way to a new land. Its eerie spirit trees grew steadily larger as the beach of the north reservation drew closer.

Forty minutes after they had left Suqua, Tony thrust the canoe up onto the sand with a mighty stroke of the paddle. A path had been cleared up the steep, vine-covered bank where moldy blackberries still hung among the thorns.

Tony handed Ida a basket filled with cans of beans and tomatoes, took several bundles himself, and started off. Little Grandma and Mother followed, their tools clanking in their arms as they walked.

The trail circled the edge of the Tilman allotment. No smoke rose from the chimney of the house partially hidden by mist and trees. "The senior Tilmans must still be at the cannery," Tony said over his shoulder to Ida.

"Must be," agreed Ida. She remembered with uneasi-ness Deaf Ellington's chilling story last year of coming upon the half-drowned Tilman boys floundering in the water after capsizing on their way home from school one day. After that their worried parents had sent them to boarding school at Tulalip.

Putting the picture out of her mind, Ida hurried to catch up with Tony, who had disappeared into the woods ahead. She nearly ran into him where the path made a turn in the dim, damp grove of cedars. He had stopped short.

Ida peered around him to see what was in the way. Stretched across the path was a beautiful spider's web, silvery with dew. "The web of life," Tony whispered to her.

He pointed to first one strand and then another. "Here is Ida. Here is Tony. Here are all the others heading towards the same center, all connected along the way.

"And here are the teardrops." He shook a branch that held the web, and dew rained down from the strands. "The teardrops are little sadnesses that come from being connected," he said. He ducked under the web and continued on. Ida followed with a backward glance at the interwoven strands.

A few more turns and the path opened onto a meadow where Father's white tent was barely visible in the grey mist. Nearby, a bumpy, half-finished log house looked like a creature rising from a marsh.

Father came around the corner of the house. "My wheel turner has come!" he said. He gave Ida a hug and then went down the trail to meet Mother.

"How do you get in?" Ida asked Tony, looking around the corners of the house. "Where's the door?"

"There isn't going to be one," said Tony. "You have to get in through the roof."

Ida frowned at him for teasing her.

"Wait. Just wait," he said. "The window and door holes will be cut after the windows and doors have been bought."

Mother reached the clearing then and exclaimed over how large the house looked. She walked all around it with Father, saying, "Here is the kitchen—we'll put the stove against this wall.... Here is the front room with a window on either side of the door.... Ida and Grandma's bedroom is here, with the bed along the back wall, and here is our bedroom.... The morning sun will come through the window. Lovely."

Father looked very pleased. He said that he and Tony would take another day or so to finish the walls. Then they would have to hurry to get the roof on.

He pointed out a small pile of cedar shingles he had split for the roof. "We won't have time to get the cracks between the logs filled. And we'll wait to cut the door and windows when we need them."

"When are we going to move?" Ida asked nervously.

"Not until we have to," said Father.

Little Grandma began poking around the garden area with a stick, breaking up chunks of charred stump that Tony and Father had dynamited and burned.

All the logs had been cleared away from the garden and four corner posts set. "You don't really need a fence out here," Tony told Grandma. "There are no sheep, and deer will jump anything you put up. But we thought you might like one anyway. We'll build it later."

Little Grandma nodded appreciatively. Then everyone set to a task. Tony worked stripping limbs from logs yet to be placed. Father trimmed shingles, Mother gathered kindling in order to be near Father, and Ida helped Grandma dig rocks and level the garden.

By noon the mist had turned to drizzle. Everyone crowded shivering into the tent to eat. Ida wished there were a fire to warm her feet. Mother reluctantly agreed with Father that it would be best for her and Ida and Grandma to return home, given the look of the skies.

On the way back to the canoe, Ida imagined herself setting off for school each day on this path. Again, she thought of the Tilman boys trying to get home across the bay. She stepped off into the brush and waited for Mother, who was coming behind her. "Mother," she asked, "how am I going to get to school?"

"We don't know yet," said Mother. "Maybe you will go over with the Miltons."

"That would be fine," said Ida with relief. But then she remembered— "Mr. Milton only comes in good weather, Mother."

"As he should. You can do lessons at home the other days."

"In winter, it's mostly bad weather," murmured Ida. She fell into step behind Mother. "Maybe *you* could take me, Mother," she said. "On your way to work."

"I won't travel that far in bad weather, either," Mother said over her shoulder. "That's why I will not be going to work on the island once we move."

Ida sighed. She had to admit, though, that grownups, as well as children, could capsize in rough water. "But what are you going to do at home, Mother?" she asked.

"I am going to work on the new house."

That seemed to Ida a better idea than doing other people's laundry when you already had to do your own at home. "You can keep Little Grandma company, too," she added.

Going over with Mr. Milton was all right, she decided. At least she wouldn't have to stay home *every* day like Mother and Little Grandma. In good weather, when the water was calm, she could be with the other children.

Tony remained working on the allotment while Father paddled the family back to Suqua, staying only long enough to unload them on the beach. He promised to return the following Friday for supper. On Sunday he would have to leave for logging camp.

Ida had temporarily forgotten about that. Father would be gone again for an entire month. She already minded it more than she ever had before. Soggy and dejected, she lumbered up the slope with Mother and Little Grandma.

Chapter 11

Superintendent's Orders

November brought rainy skies that asked nothing of anyone. Neighbors who had, in October, lingered on doorsteps to exchange words about progress on their allotments, now withdrew inside.

At school the children straggled in wet and chilled. They hovered around the barrel stove and put their damp shoes beneath it to dry. The classroom smelled of steaming leather.

Most days it was too wet to go outside for recess. The weather suppressed even Leroy, who wandered about only half-heartedly annoying others. In the lunch shack the children lingered unenthusiastically over their lukewarm dinners.

Ida came down with a runny nose and then a cough. Grandma, who fearlessly wore no shoes most of the winter, worried that the cough would turn to pneumonia.

She considered pneumonia the same as smallpox—a direct route to death. She kept Ida tucked into Mother's bed in the front room for several days, coaxing her into drinking teas and broths.

When Ida complained about taking them, Mother said, "In the old days your family would have made a bed for you outdoors so the rain would wash away your sickness."

"Is that true, Grandma?" asked Ida.

"Maybe," said Grandma.

"You wouldn't let them do that to me," Ida said confidently.

Grandma smiled.

Ida passed the time in bed paging through a lovely leather dictionary Father had bought in Seattle the year before. She liked best the words that had little pictures by them. In the "C's" she learned what caribou, castanets, and catapults were.

In the "P's" she found palette, Patagonia, and without any picture, potlatch, "a gathering of North Pacific Coast Indians in which a distribution of gifts takes place." The dictionary itself had come to the family through a potlatch. A man Father knew from another tribe had given away all his money, asking that it be spent on reminders of his son who had died while away at law school.

Father knew the son had possessed a good knowledge of words, so he had purchased this book with the money given him at the potlatch. He hoped Ida, too, would learn about words. She wondered now what the son had died of.

At last the day came when Grandma allowed her to return to school. She had to wear an old-time, cone-shaped rainhat made of woven cedar bark as she went down the path in the drizzle.

Katie was pleased by her return. She coughed and looked feverish herself, but was unwilling to stay home. She missed enough school just taking care of her sisters and brother.

"It's been very dull without you," she whispered. "Nothing but boys."

By afternoon recess the sun was making a brave attempt, and the boys dashed out to take advantage of it. Katie and Ida followed more slowly, squeezing past Teacher's wife in the doorway as she brought in the mail.

"Letter from Tulalip," said Katie, recognizing the

return address stamped on the top envelope. "The superintendent wants to know how many of us have died of rain this month." She and Ida giggled.

"When are you moving to your place?" Katie asked as they walked down to the water.

"Not until we have to," said Ida. "It's not finished yet."

"Maybe you'll never have to move. Maybe we'll all be able to stay here like always," said Katie.

"I don't think so."

"Maybe, Ida," Katie said earnestly. "Maybe."

Ida wished that it were so, but Father would not have built the new house if her family did not need to move. Teacher had said they must get established on their allotment or risk losing it.

She thought of Nellie Goldsmith's vow to stay on the beach, even if they built the fort over her. Katie's family had already lived on their allotment on the south reservation when Katie's father was still around. They did not have to fear losing their land now, even if they did not live there.

Ida slipped her arm around Katie's waist. "We can still be together at school, Katie, no matter what."

Katie sighed. "At least we have that."

She and Ida linked arms and strolled along the beach.

Teacher was unusually quiet after calling the students in. Even Leroy noticed. He glanced at the letter lying open on Teacher's desk. "It's not about Tulalip, is it?" he asked. "I still get to go, don't I? You said I could!"

"Take your seat, Leroy," Teacher said.

Leroy did as he was told, looking very worried.

Katie eyed the letter with suspicion.

Ida smiled at her confidently. It did not matter to them whether or not Leroy was allowed to go to Tulalip, though of course things would be nicer if he did.

When everyone was seated, Teacher picked up the letter and went to the dictionary stand. Resting his arms on the book, he leaned forward to speak. "As you know," he began, "the law requires all children between five and eighteen to be in regular attendance at school." His eyes scanned the empty seats in the room.

"Two-thirds of our students are absent today. Some of them are sick from walking to school in the rain. Some live too far away to get here easily. Others, of course, have stayed away because they do not care to learn."

Katie looked out of the corner of her eye at Ida. Ida looked at Simon. Simon shrugged and looked at Leroy.

What was Teacher getting at? Did anybody know? Everyone listened carefully, trying to pick up an early clue from Teacher's words.

With a troubled look, Teacher rubbed a hand against his forehead. "On reservations where there is a boarding school, these problems do not exist—for the most part," he added. "Since we are not so fortunate as to have a boarding school here at Port Madison, we must take advantage of the one at Tulalip."

Leroy turned and beamed a reassuring smile to his classmates. No one smiled back.

"As I told you in September, the superintendent has reserved fifteen spaces at Tulalip for Port Madison students. I have spoken to some of your parents about this opportunity. So far only two spaces have been reserved, in addition to those taken by Tom Flanders and the two Tilmans."

Leroy waved his hand in the air. "My brother won't be able to go, Teacher. He's seeing the doctor in Seattle for tuberculosis."

"As I feared," said Teacher. With a sigh he studied the letter one more time and then looked over his students. In an apologetic voice he said, "The superintendent has found it necessary to assign the remaining spaces to students he feels will most benefit from the opportunity at Tulalip."

A shudder rippled through the classroom.

Teacher quickly continued. "The forced move from Suqua has determined some of the assignments. Because of the distance you must travel to school, those of you on the north reservation will go to Tulalip. That would be the Miltons and Ida."

Katie gasped.

Ida felt as though she herself had swallowed a clamshell.

Teacher shook his head sadly and went on. "In addition the superintendent expects to see Simon, Ramon, Robert, Maggie, George, and Thomas Bonneville. Also–"

The Bonneville children looked stunned.

"Me, Teacher, don't forget me," said Leroy nervously.

"Leroy makes thirteen, and there are two spaces left." Katie shook her head.

"I could go," offered her little brother.

"No, Daniel," Teacher said quietly. "I will need

you and your family to help fill the new school here."

You need me, too! Ida tried to say the words, but her mouth would not work.

Teacher set the letter on his desk, under the paper-weight. "First-level arithmetic, take your place at the blackboard. Level-four readers, begin the story on page twenty-three. Daniel—"

"But I'm coming to school with Mr. Milton!" Ida choked out at last. "Mathew and Rose and I are coming to the new school *here.*"

"Ida, Mr. Milton is going to be working in Port Gamble this winter."

Ida's eyes blurred with tears. "But maybe my mother—"

"Ida, you cannot cross in bad weather. There is much bad weather in winter. This is a chance for you to get a better education than I can give you here."

"Teacher, when do we have to go?" said Leroy, a little more somber now that he seemed to sense the mood of the class.

"I forgot to say, didn't I? Not till after Christmas. Treaty Day is when the term will open. January twenty-second, Treaty Day." He beckoned the arithmetic group with his hand. "Daniel, copy over yesterday's corrected composition."

Katie put an arm around Ida's shoulder and gave her a squeeze. "You can come and live with me," she whispered fiercely.

Tears spilled down Ida's cheeks. Her nose began to run, too.

Teacher looked very sorry. He pulled out his handkerchief and handed it to Ida.

Chapter 12

Little Grandma's Tears

The long afternoon was finally over. Leroy raced out of the schoolyard with the news. Ida toiled up the slope with the weight of a giant stone inside her. It seemed she would never get home to Little Grandma.

When she finally reached the house, she found it empty. She went outside and called for Grandma from the doorstep. She called for her in the woods behind the house. Where was Grandma? She needed her!

She walked back along the path in front of the church, her eyes scanning the beach below. No one was out. It occurred to her that Grandma might have gone to fill the water baskets. She could not remember if she had seen them inside the door.

Hurrying now, she slipped and slid along the muddy

path to the stream. The wet brush along the way soaked her dress and stockings. At the last turn before the stream she heard a moaning noise.

"Ah-de-dah, ah-de-dah."

She stopped short. That was Grandma's voice! Frightened, she forced her eyes to search the bushes on either side of the path. She made each foot lift up and move forward, closer to the sound.

She spotted Grandma just beyond the turn, sitting on the flat stone beside the stream bed. Little Grandma rocked back and forth moaning. It took Ida a moment to realize it was not an injury that caused Little Grandma's distress. Grandma's face glistened with tears.

"Ah-de-dah, ah-de-dah." Little Grandma was weeping.

Ida was so shocked that when she could finally move, she whirled around and ran back down the trail into Suqua calling, "David! David Jennings! Something terrible has happened to Grandma!"

David could not understand her above the barking of his roused dogs. He motioned her into the house and shut the door.

"Little Grandma is crying, David!" Ida said breathlessly. "She's crying by the stream!"

David looked as though he might cry, too. "Guk-kub has much sadness right now," he said. "Too many changes. Today Mr. Simpson's wife tells her they send her granddaughter far away."

Ida swallowed hard. Grandma had already heard her news.

"We cry. We all cry," David said beside her. "Sometimes inside, sometimes outside. We cry when we cannot change what happens. When we cannot help our little ones."

Tears rolled down Ida's cheeks.

David wiped them away with his thumb. "Your mother comes soon," he said. He took her hand in his, and they peered out the dusty window at the Sound.

Around the point of the island a speck grew gradually larger, until they could clearly see that the lone paddler was Mother. Ida opened the door and ran to meet her.

Mother smiled tiredly as she stepped from the canoe. Before she could even pull it up on the sand, Ida blurted out, "Teacher says I have to go to Tulalip boarding school, Mother! Grandma is crying."

Mother looked startled. "Where is Grandma now?"

"At the stream."

"You go home. I will see to Grandma." She pulled the canoe onto the beach and hurried up the slope alongside Ida. At the church they went in opposite directions.

Ida arrived at home so weary she could hardly push open the door. She made her way to Grandma's chair and sat down, setting the chair in slow, rhythmic motion.

Rocking did not make her feel better. Nothing so terrible as this had ever happened before. Little Grandma crying. The superintendent sending her away. She wanted Mother. She wanted her *now*.

When the door finally opened and Mother came in alone, Ida slid from the chair and ran into her arms. "I can't go to Tulalip!" she said. "If I go away, Little Grandma will die!"

"Lo, lo—Grandma is stronger than that," said Mother. "She has had disappointments before." Mother hung up her coat and set the coffeepot to heat on the stove.

"But not like this one," said Ida.

"Worse than this one," said Mother. She sat tiredly down at the table and rested her head in her hands. Ida came and leaned against the chair to be closer to her.

Mother glanced at her. "I will tell you about the worst one that happened. It was when Grandma was living happily with her husband and her little girl among the Twana. Her husband's other wife and her three little children lived with them."

"His other wife?" said Ida.

"He had two," said Mother. "One day a law was passed saying Indians could have only one. Grandma's husband did not want to give up either of his wives, so he was put in jail. Grandma decided she must leave. She came back to Suqua. It was very hard."

"Did she cry?" asked Ida.

"She did not," said Mother. "She was strong."

"She cried on the inside," said Ida sadly. "What happened to her little girl?"

Mother took a deep breath. "Before Grandma left, she went to her daughter, who was at the boarding school on the reservation, and said, 'Today we are going away. Go to the jail to say goodbye to your father. Go to the house where your brothers and sister and your other mother wait to see you for the last time.'"

Ida looked at Mother's face. Her chin was tipped up, like Little Grandma's had been at fishing camp when she told about leaving her family.

"The little girl did as she was told," said Mother. "Her tears were so many that she could hardly see where she was going. She said goodbye to everyone; then she and Grandma came away." Mother's eyes glistened. She got up and poured herself a cup of coffee.

Ida was still. Mother had been that little girl. "I could not do that," she said.

Mother poked a knife into a can of beans and began to cut the lid off to prepare for supper. "We all do what we have to," she said. "Grandma and I carried on, and so will you."

Ida was not convinced or comforted, either.

When Grandma came in, Ida put an arm around her waist and pressed her cheek to hers. Grandma held her close.

They ate supper silently, too affected by feelings to talk. As soon as Mother finished the dishes, they all went to bed, worn out by the strains of the day.

Although Ida snuggled up to Grandma as she always did, she could not fall asleep. She was scared. More scared than she had ever been before.

Despite what Mother said, she knew she would *not*

be able to carry on at Tulalip. Mother did not know how it was. She had not had to leave home all by herself. Only Little Grandma knew. And Little Grandma had *cried* for her.

If only Mother would refuse to let her go, like Nellie had with Katie. But she knew, with a terrible pinch in her stomach, that Mother would not protest.

As Grandma snored wearily beside her, she felt like a little stove cast into the deepest part of the Sound.

The next day dawned gloomy and wet like most of November before it. Ida wordlessly accepted the rain hat from Grandma before leaving the house. She went slowly down the slope feeling that she was a different person from the girl she had been the day before.

She arrived early at the schoolhouse and, pushing open the door, found only Leroy there. He stood at the front of the room studying the map of the state of Washington.

She tried not to attract his attention as she slid past Katie's seat to her own. No heat came from the barrel stove yet, despite the smoke seeping from around its door. She tucked her hands in her coat pockets. It was with relief that she heard the sound of approaching voices outside.

Leroy also heard them and sprang into action. He soon had the new arrivals gathered around the map. "Here is Tulalip," he said, using Teacher's pointer. "We're down here at Suqua. Here's Seattle. Like a triangle, see? And way over here is the Pacific Ocean." He glanced Ida's way.

She ignored him.

"Now, my father says it takes two days to get to Tulalip by canoe," he said importantly. "But we could take the steamer over to Seattle and catch a train up to Marysville." He outlined the journey with the pointer. "Probably they would send a carriage to take us from the train station to the school."

None of the children had ever ridden on a train before or even seen one up close. As for a carriage—those were for important people. The children looked at Leroy with new respect.

"The superintendent will determine how you are to get to Tulalip," said Teacher, who had come in unobserved. "Take your seats," he ordered.

Two whole days to Tulalip? Ida busied herself at her desk as though she had not been listening herself.

That was as far as to Cousin Magda's. Father would never let her go that far away. Father would want her to stay close by the reservation so that he could see her when he came home. Surely Father would not let her go to Tulalip.

Chapter 13

The Bonnevilles Pack Up

That evening Mother began to talk cautiously about what it would be like at boarding school. "You will have many friends your own age," she said to Ida. "You might like that."

"I only need Katie," murmured Ida.

"Cousin Magda likes boarding school," said Mother.

"Aunt and Uncle see her every week," said Ida. "Would you come to see me every week?"

"Tulalip is much further away," said Mother. "I would send you letters."

Ida was too unhappy to speak.

On Saturday morning she watched Mother leave for work in the cold drizzle. Little Grandma went out for her bath. Ida wandered down to the beach to look out for Father even though it was not the weekend for him to come home.

The beach was a solitary place now. Everyone stayed

inside hunched over their stoves. She stood in the door-way of Tony's shack, out of the damp. Tony had not been around for several days. He had brought his water basket to Ida to care for.

In winter, when his shack was impossible to keep warm, he made a circuit of his relatives. He might be over at Tracyton with his uncle now or in Lemolo with cousins or maybe at his sister's near Miller's Bay.

Ida scanned the water all the way up the beach past Katie's house. She allowed herself to hope that Father had already heard the news and was coming home early to do something about it. But there was no boat coming from Dogfish Bay and none from any other direction, either.

She wished again that Father would give up logging and become a farmer. Then he would be home to take her back and forth to school every day. He would be sitting at the supper table every night. And she would be sitting in the classroom with Katie when Leroy went off to Tulalip.

"Why didn't you build a fire?" asked a voice beside her.

Ida shied like a spooked horse. "Tony!"

"I suppose I'm all out of wood," he said, grinning guiltily. He put an arm around her to keep her warm. "Why are you out fishing for pneumonia?" he scolded.

Ida took a deep breath. "Teacher says I have to go to Tulalip!"

"Tulalip Indian School?"

Ida nodded.

"So you're running away?"

Ida scowled at him. "I'm watching for Father."

"Hmmmm." Tony looked to the southwest. "A little soon for him to be coming, isn't it? You know I went to boarding school—St. George's—for a while. Remember when I did that? You get to come home in summer, you know."

Ida was not impressed. "Children die at boarding school."

"Children die on the reservations, too," said Tony. "When do you have to go?"

"January twenty-second."

Tony turned her shoulders to face him. "I'll tell you what," he said. "I'll come back to see you off when it's time to go. Would you like that?"

Ida nodded.

"Count on me, then."

He went inside and unloaded rumpled laundry from his pack. Ida watched him take a pair of pants and a blue flannel shirt down from a nail and stuff them in the pack to replenish his wardrobe. Then, reshouldering his load, he tipped his city hat to her and headed west in the direction of Lemolo, three miles away.

When Tony had disappeared from view, Ida borrowed the army blanket from his cot and settled herself outside in a beached canoe. She imagined herself paddling to Dogfish Bay on her way to Father's logging camp. She might never return.

No matter what Tony or anybody else said, she did not want to go to Tulalip. Grandma didn't want her to go, either. Nobody could ever come to see her there.

It was still drizzling, and she began to shiver despite the blanket. She was just about to climb out and go home when, a stone's throw down the beach, the door to the Bonneville house opened.

The Bonneville children had not returned to school since Teacher had named them to go to Tulalip. It was as though they feared being trapped in the schoolhouse and hauled away.

Now the family filed out of their small house, one by one, each with an armload of possessions that they piled on the beach beside their old war-sized canoe. Carl Bonneville and his older sons began to take apart the house, starting with the cedar shingles on the roof.

Ida remembered their having done this once before, when they had gone away for several months. It would take only a couple of hours. Their house was so small she had always wondered how they could all live inside it. Certainly their canoe would never have fit into it!

She wondered where they were going now. They were all so somber that it did not seem proper to ask.

The roof done, Carl and his sons began on the walls, carefully prying off the planks and stacking them in the middle half of the canoe. Mrs. Bonneville had already settled herself in one end with two windows balanced on her lap. Two of the children sat atop the shingles, while the youngest peered out from the pile of bedding on the beach.

The last wall was nearly apart when Teacher hurried across the sand. "It's too bad it's come to this, Bonneville," he said to Carl. "It's the law that says your children have to go to school, not me. You can't escape that no matter where you go."

"School here, yes — Tulalip, no," said Carl.

"Your children hardly come to school now living right next to the schoolhouse. The superintendent knows they would come even less often from your allotment. That's why he wants them at Tulalip."

Carl went on pulling off planking.

Teacher frowned and looked towards the children in the canoe.

Ida tried to make herself small so that no one would think she was there to watch.

Teacher's voice was angry when he turned back to Carl. "You realize, Bonneville, that you'll lose your land, leaving the reservation like this. I can't hold that land for you. It'll be free for jumping."

Carl took an armload of lumber to the canoe.

Teacher turned his hands up in a sign that he was helpless to do anything about the situation. With his forehead deeply wrinkled by concern, he tromped back to his house.

Simon hurried back from Deaf Ellington's with a shovel and began to dig out the corner posts. These, too, were hauled to the canoe.

The boys finished packing the household goods around the building supplies and squeezed into the heavily laden canoe. Carl returned the shovel before taking his place among his family. All that was left on the beach was a pile of rubbish and the ashes from the stove.

As Carl and his sons thrust their paddles into the water, Ida wanted to cry out, "Wait for me, I'm coming, too!" but she could not find her voice. The canoe was several lengths from shore before she even raised her hand in goodbye.

Simon was the only one facing in her direction. He was busy helping his youngest brother pee over the side of the boat and could not wave back.

Chapter 14

As Long As We Can

All of Ida's watching did not bring Father home any sooner than expected. She went to bed Thanksgiving Eve imagining him starting for Suqua the way he had described to her many times when she was small.

First he would rest in the bunkhouse for a few hours after his day's work. Then he would get up in the dark and make the long walk from Hood Canal to Dogfish Bay. He said he knew the trail so well that if he wanted to, he could close his eyes and finish sleeping as he walked. At Dogfish Bay he would get in his canoe and paddle past Keyport and around the point to Suqua.

He would arrive at dawn. Ida planned to be on the beach to meet him. She wanted to tell him herself all that had gone wrong while he had been away.

Mother and Little Grandma might think Ida must go to Tulalip, but Father would know how to prevent that from happening.

Before she went to bed, she drank three cupfuls of water. She had heard Leroy tell Katie's little brother that such a quantity of water would make a person wake up early with the need to pee. That was how warriors woke themselves up to go on raids at dawn, he said.

Ida was awakened the next morning by a window filled with hazy sunlight. The only thing drinking all that extra water had done was to give her nightmares about waves crashing over her.

In her bare feet she dashed out through the icy morning dew to the outhouse. On the way back she saw a deer carcass hanging in the woodshed. Father was home!

She was sorry she had missed the chance to talk to him alone, but he was *here*. That was the important thing. Now she could stop worrying.

All morning Father slept in the bed in the front room, his mouth half-open, making little snorting noises every third breath. When he snored, Ida thought, he looked as old as David Jennings.

Mother and Little Grandma moved about quietly

and purposefully. They baked bread, then an apple pie, then squash, one at a time, in the covered kettle on top of the ovenless stove.

"Now can I wake him?" Ida asked Mother for the fourth time.

"No, you can set the table," said Mother.

Making as much noise as possible, Ida pulled a large basket out from under Father's bed. She set the lid aside and took out the lovely handwoven cream-colored tablecloth and napkins that Mother's Twana grandmother had sent for Mother's wedding day.

Folded neatly under the tablecloth were Father's city clothes and Mother's blue city dress. Under the clothes were their good shoes wrapped in brown paper.

Ida slid the basket back under the bed, giving the frame a little bump. She thought she saw Father's eyelids flicker.

Grandma helped her straighten the cloth on the table, and together they set out the silverware and plates and matching napkins. At the head of each plate, in a clamshell, Grandma placed dried fruit—apple, plum, pear, and berries—to acknowledge the bounty of water and land.

"David Jennings will be here very soon, Mother," Ida warned.

Mother lifted the lid on the venison stew and tasted it with a spoon. Ida could not see how Father could possibly sleep with all those delicious smells drifting around him. "Now you can wake him," Mother said.

Ida hurried to the bed. She put her hands on Father's thick upper arms, red in flannel long johns. "Father!" she said, giving him a little shake.

Father mumbled. Ida teased him with another shake. Suddenly Father's hands shot out and grabbed her around the waist, hoisting her up in the air over the bed.

Ida screeched. She had the strongest father in the world! All too soon he set her back on her feet and sat up, shaking the sleep from his head.

When he learned the time, he leapt from bed and climbed into the clean clothes Mother had laid out for him. Quickly, he washed his face and combed his hair.

He had hardly emptied the wash basin out the door when David Jennings appeared with an offering of smoked fish and a paper cone of sweets. "Have I come to the right cooking fire?" he asked.

"Your place is here," said Little Grandma.

Soon dinner was set out, and Father said a blessing. They all made the sign of the cross, saying, "In the name of the Father, the Son, and the Holy Spirit, Amen."

Ida looked over the table with satisfaction. There was the rich, orange-brown venison stew, squash and potatoes from Grandma's garden, plum jam and bread, spiced pears, and pie. They could eat for days and never finish. No one spoke for several minutes while they sampled each tasty dish.

"May the women of the house live long and well," said David Jennings at last.

"And the men in turn," replied Mother.

Only pleasant subjects were spoken of. By late afternoon the table had long been cleared of all but the clamshells and empty coffee cups. Everyone stretched out for a nap except David Jennings, who rested in Grandma's rocking chair with a piece of firewood for a footrest.

Ida was the first one to get up. She fidgeted with the clamshells and tried not to think about Tulalip. As dusk came on, everyone gathered back at the table for a final cup of coffee.

David Jennings looked around the circle, his eyes

pausing longest on Ida. He sighed and said, "If we understood the white man better in the beginning, we would have outsmarted them."

Everyone waited for David to explain what he was thinking. "They push us here, they push us there," he said. "Now they take our children."

Ida glanced at Father. Had Mother told him about the superintendent's orders? Father looked at Mother. He took up a small piece of driftwood and began to whittle it.

"You speak the truth, David," he said. "But in order to learn how the paesteds think, our children must go to school. If we do not educate them, they will be taken advantage of."

"But the children go away!" said David. "The paesteds separate all our people! What will we be without our children?"

Ida waited for Father to say that the children would not have to go away. But he did not do that. "We will keep our children with us as long as we can," he said.

Ida swung her legs nervously under the table. Why wasn't Father more hopeful? She glanced at David Jennings. He reached over and patted her on the arm.

"I, myself, am a tired child," he said to the others, getting up stiffly from his chair. "I have had a pleasant afternoon, and now my bed calls me."

Mother smiled at him affectionately and brought his coat. All the family went to the door to see him off.

Chapter 15

Wishful Thinking

At breakfast the next morning Father was silent. Ida knew not to interrupt him when he was deep in thought. She almost shook with the desire to tell him she really could not go to Tulalip.

Finally he said to Mother, "If we were to move off the reservation, Ida could go to a paested school close to home. She might find herself unwelcome there, though. And we would lose the allotment."

Ida held her breath. Did she want to go to a white-man school?

Father continued. "We could acquire land off the reservation by homesteading. But homesteads must be farmed. That is the law. I am not a farmer." He looked at Mother apologetically.

"You are not a farmer," Mother agreed. She began to clear away the breakfast dishes.

"There is talk of changing the law so that allotments

can be sold to outsiders," he said, thinking out loud. "By selling the allotment we could buy a house somewhere and not have to farm." He gazed through the window across the room.

Mother remained silent.

"If we begin to sell off the reservation, though, it will be the end of the Suquamish," he argued unhappily. "Now it is only the land that can keep us together as a people. We must hold onto it!" He unexpectedly brought his fist down on the table. Ida flinched.

"Maybe Ida could go to St. George's," Mother said quietly.

Father looked at her quickly.

St. George's? thought Ida. Magda?

"That would be better than Tulalip," Father agreed. "Just as far away, but she would have family there. My brother would keep watch over her. I will talk to Mr. Simpson."

He put on his coat and went out the door.

"St. George's *would* be better, Mother," Ida said with hesitation. "But I want to stay here."

Mother said brusquely, "The superintendent is unlikely to allow that, even if you *could* get to school every day. He seems to have his mind made up and may not allow you to go to St. George's, either." She plunged the breakfast dishes into the dishpan with a clatter.

Ida had never seen Mother so vexed. Was she vexed with *her?* Or could it be with the superintendent? This was the closest she had ever seen Mother come to making a fuss.

Little Grandma came out of the back room and, sitting down by the stove, began to work on a new basket.

Ida sidled over to the steamed-up window and wiped it clear with her sleeve to keep a watch out for Father. She could see just a small section of the beach — Tony's deserted shack and the empty space where the Bonnevilles' house had stood. Across the way, fog drifted from the island out to the Sound.

Behind her, Mother said rapidly, under her breath, "At Tulalip, all the children are from the Tribes. It is not so far away as Chemawa in Oregon. Nellie's sisters went to Chemawa. They did not come back."

The strange nervousness in her voice made Ida uneasy. "Sadie Morrison over at Tracyton is sending her daughters to Tulalip. She thinks it a very good opportunity for them to get ahead." Mother threw the dishwater out the door. With determination, she thrust the laundry tub on the table and filled it with hot water from the stove.

It was not long before Ida spotted Father. He did not smile or even seem to notice her in the window as he turned in at the gate. When he reached the doorstep, Ida quietly opened the door for him.

Mother dried her hands and set the coffeepot to heat. Father hung up his coat.

Little Grandma paused in her work.

"Ida may not go to St. George's to be with Magda," Father said. "The superintendent expects the children of this district to go to the new school he has built for them in Tulalip."

Ida sank back against the wall.

"But what about the Henson children?" protested Mother. "*They* go to St. George's!"

"Mr. Simpson says students already enrolled there may continue, though the superintendent does not like it."

Mother sat down at the table with a dazed look on her face. It was clear then to Ida that despite Mother's talk, she had hoped all along to keep Ida from having to go to Tulalip.

Father put his arm around Mother. "No one knew when the Treaty promised schools that it would come to this," he murmured.

Ida turned away from them. They could not help her. This was a thousand times worse than losing Suqua. Now, she was losing her family. Noiselessly, she moved towards the door and slipped outside. With steps neither fast nor slow she walked through Grandma's sleeping garden, out the gate, and past the churchyard.

She kept her eyes on the path, turning down into Suqua, past the school surrounded by jagged apple trees, and on past Teacher's house, soon to be abandoned.

Her jaws grew tight with cold. She had come away without her coat. At water's edge she turned west and followed the beach to Katie's house. Smoke erupted from its chimney in fitful starts, and the place seemed strangely quiet.

She listened at the door a moment, then pushed it open hesitantly. Inside the one-room shack, Katie stood at a table picking meat from a chicken carcass. She looked up in surprise. "Ida!" she whispered. "What are you doing here?"

Ida glanced at the beds along the walls, each filled with sleeping shapes—here Nellie's large one, there several smaller ones. Someone breathed through a stuffed-up nose, someone else whimpered in her sleep. Ida had forgotten how crowded the house was.

Nellie coughed like an old man. Ida mouthed the word "sick?"

"Since Tuesday," whispered Katie. "You better not stay." She dumped the bits of meat into a pot on the little stove that heated the room, then came to the door. Taking her mother's shawl from a hook, she stepped outside with Ida and closed the door behind them. "What did you want?" she asked.

Ida felt her throat suddenly close. Why had she come? Katie's declaration that she must stay with her instead of going to Tulalip had only been wishful thinking. There was no room at Katie's house for another person. Nellie could hardly take care of her own children.

No, Katie could not help her. How could she, when Father himself had not been able to. "I have to go to Tulalip," was all she could think to say.

"I know," said Katie. She wrapped Ida into the shelter of the shawl with her. "You're lucky. You'll be able to study with the other children every day, no matter what. You'll wear nice, ironed uniforms and eat at a table with lots of food three times a day. And sing and have celebrations."

Ida looked at the ground where Katie's bare feet sought each other for warmth and her own brown button shoes waited uncertainly. She wanted to say, Come with me, Katie. But she already knew that Katie could not be spared from home.

Katie choked down a sob. "I'll miss you, Ida."

They embraced tightly. Then Katie pulled away and went inside.

Chapter 16

The Basket Dolls

Sunday morning, before Father went back to logging camp, he took Ida out in the canoe. Near Miller's Bay he drew in his paddle and lowered a fishing line. He and Ida sat in silence for a long while, Ida too miserable to talk, Father deep in thought.

At last he looked down into the water and said, "Separations are a part of life, daughter. Some of them come much sooner than we are ready for, but no one escapes them."

Ida's eyes filled with tears. Father understood about the terrible weight inside her. She began to shake with sobs. Father reached over and lifted her chin with his rough fingers.

"No one can take away what is already part of us. I will think about you at Tulalip. You will think about us here. You will be a daughter of Suqua always, no matter what happens to Suqua itself."

Ida looked into his dark eyes filled with concern and slowly wiped away her tears.

Father rebaited a hook for her, and they fished a while longer.

In bed that night, long after Father had gone, Ida nestled against Grandma and sighed deeply. Grandma reached back and gave her a loving pat. "The sun, too, knows darkness," she murmured. "Still, it goes on rising."

The following afternoon Little Grandma set aside the basket she had started. With narrow strips cut from cattail leaves she began to weave what looked like a thumb. Ida had seen her make that shape only twice before.

"Grandma, who are you making that doll for?" she asked.

"For someone going far away," said Little Grandma without looking up.

"For Rose?" asked Ida.

"For someone going with Rose," said Grandma.

Ida went into the back room and took from a shelf two dolls, a mother doll and a father doll. Woven in the way baskets were, each was no larger than her hand. Back in the front room, she settled on Mother and Father's bed with the dolls in her lap.

Grandma continued working after supper. By bedtime little grey and black braids, a tiny nose, and the rest of a face sitting atop a fat grandma bosom had emerged from Grandma's labors.

In the evenings that followed, Little Grandma wove a skirt with a border of tiny salmon around the bottom. When the grandma doll was finished, she started on a girl doll.

December moved quickly along as though to keep itself warm. Teacher and his wife bustled about, cheerful at the prospect of being in their new house on the hill by Christmas.

The rest of Suqua was more subdued. With glum faces people watched Teacher direct his students up the slope carrying armloads of schoolbooks and furniture. Soon the abandoned school and teacher's empty house were undeniable signs of change.

Everyone else seemed determined to stay until the army arrived on the beach to extract them. Work on the allotments had slowed considerably with the return of the rainy season. Mother hoped she would not have to move into the unfinished house on the north reservation before Ida left for Tulalip.

She began to sew a going-away dress for Ida from material she had asked Annie Ellington to bring back from Seattle. Every evening after supper she set her sewing machine on the table and turned the crank that made the needle go up and down, up and down in the material. Ida stood beside her and watched the stitches form like little paddle strokes.

"How many strokes do you think it takes to get to Tulalip?" she asked.

Mother half-smiled. "A great many. Probably you will not be going by canoe, though. Mr. Simpson says the school will send a motor launch. Maybe it would only take four or five hours."

"You could come and visit me in a motor launch," said Ida hopefully.

Mother touched her forehead to Ida's. "I wish I *had* a motor launch," she said.

Christmas came. It was the last time Ida would see Father for a long, long time. She would leave for Tulalip before he came back again. He brought her a piece of driftwood he had carved into a little canoe the exact shape of his own, even with a gash in its side.

Little Grandma placed the grandmother doll and the girl doll with their matching salmon skirts inside the canoe. Ida brought out the mother and father dolls and put them in as well. "We'll all go to Tulalip," she said wistfully.

Grandma shook her head. "They don't let me go to school at Tulalip," she said. Her eyes twinkled. "No English," she added, speaking English for the very first time.

Everyone laughed, even Ida.

That afternoon Father Marguine, the Catholic priest whose home church was at Tulalip, came across from Seattle to say an evening mass. After supper Ida and her family filed into the little mission church along with almost everyone else in Suqua.

Cedar boughs strung along the pews filled the room with the fresh scent of the forest. Candles in the windows and on the table altar bravely pushed back the shadows.

Tony arrived, dressed in his good clothes and carrying his baby nephew. "Are you ready for your trip up the Sound?" he whispered to Ida.

"Don't forget your promise," she whispered back.

She and her family knelt and stood with the others as Father Marguine's bell marked each stage of the mass. Tony's nephew was baptized. Everyone sang the offertory in Suquamish.

Afterwards Father Marguine, carrying a pitch torch, visited each home to bless it in the coming move to the allotments.

The following morning Father awakened Ida early. It was time for him to go. In the dark the two of them went down to the beach and pushed his canoe into the water. For a moment Ida imagined herself going away with him.

Father shook his head as though he had heard her thought. With the canoe rocking beside him, he said, "Five times I will not expect to see you when I come home, Daughter. On the sixth time I will paddle twice as hard, knowing you are here."

He hugged her tightly, and Ida cried into his shirt. How could she miss even one of Father's visits!

She ran along the shore as he paddled swiftly away.

The following week Teacher's new school opened. The weather was windy and wet. Teacher told Ida and Leroy they were welcome to come if they liked, or they could wait to start the new term at boarding school on the twenty-second. Rose and Mathew would be staying at home.

Ida came to work on her reading. She did not want to be behind the other children at Tulalip. Leroy decided to come, too, saying there was nothing for him to do at home.

Sometimes, while lessons were being spoken around her, Ida closed her eyes and tried to imagine how it would be to live at a school always. To eat there, to sleep there, and maybe—she was not sure about it—to play there. She wondered if the other children would notice her or be unfriendly. She tried to imagine grownups she did not know.

At night she snuggled close to Grandma and worried she would not be able to go to sleep in a bed all by herself.

Chapter 17

Treaty Day

Treaty Day approached, as unwavering as the tide. The superintendent sent word that Leroy, Ida, and the Miltons were to be at the dock at eight o'clock in the morning on the twenty-second. A Mr. Olsen from Poulsbo would be coming with his motor launch to take them to Tulalip.

"You may each bring a small basket's worth of belongings," said Teacher. "And a coat. The school will provide all the other clothing you need plus a pair of shoes."

Ida repacked her basket several times. In the bottom was a change of underwear and stockings. Then four white handkerchiefs Mother had embroidered in silver with Ida's initials. A brown paper packet of Grandma's dried fruit for the journey. Father's Christmas canoe with the dolls inside.

Leroy came by to see what she was taking with her.

She showed him everything but the stockings and the underwear.

"I'm just taking my hunting knife," he said. "What kind of food do you suppose they feed you up there at Tulalip?"

Ida had not thought about that. "Probably it will be better than what Teacher's wife cooks," she answered.

"It better be!" said Leroy. "Otherwise I might not stay." He seemed relieved just to speak with her, and Ida in turn found herself comforted by the fact that Leroy would be going, too.

"Teacher says he's still expecting Mathew and Rose," he said before he left. "But I don't know. They're awfully little to be leaving home."

Ida agreed. The younger you were, the harder it must be, she thought. It surprised her that Leroy would think of that.

The night before Treaty Day, Ida went through the house touching each wall and each door. She memorized the shapes of the little stove and the three windows that rattled in their frames when the wind blew. When she came back for the summer, she would be going to the new house.

In the back room she buried her hands in the fur lining of her cradleboard on the wall. She rubbed her face in the soft folds of a skirt of Little Grandma's hanging from a nail.

Mother appeared in the doorway and asked if Ida would like to sleep in bed with her that night. Ida said no, she would sleep with Grandma, but she went to sit in Mother's lap and stayed for a long while. She felt herself grow sleepy as Mother undid her braids and stroked her hair.

If I don't close my eyes, tomorrow won't come, she told herself. And yet she felt relieved that the waiting was almost over.

The next morning Mother delayed going to work. She made Ida pancakes with apple butter for breakfast and wrapped the extra ones for the journey.

Grandma set aside the breakfast dishes and watched as Ida and Mother got into their coats. Mother took up her rain cape and the basket and started out the door. Ida felt the stone sinking in her stomach. The time had come. She was leaving home.

She turned to Little Grandma. She must not cry. For Grandma's sake she must not. With a trembling voice, she said, "I take you with me wherever I go, Grandma."

Grandma opened her arms wide, and Ida plunged into them. "Wherever you go," whispered Grandma.

Outside, thin flurries of snow sifted down from the colorless sky as Mother closed the gate behind her and Ida. Out on the dusky water the eight o'clock steamer rounded the point of the island. Soon Mother would be paddling that way to work. From the other direction, beyond Nellie Goldsmith's shack, chugged the launch from Poulsbo.

Down on the beach, Leroy, wearing a new cap and coat, waited with his parents and his brother. Deaf Ellington and Annie came out to give support. Teacher waited close by. In a little huddle by their canoe stood the Miltons with Rose and Mathew.

Mother took Ida's hand, and they started down the slope. David Jennings's dogs set up their usual clamor as Ida and Mother passed by. David came hurrying out. He pressed a bundle of peppermint sticks into Ida's hands and looked at her tearfully.

"I will be back, David," she said, and patting his arm, walked on.

The steamer docked, and Teacher ran out for the

mail. Someone came out of the old schoolyard to join Ida and Mother.

"Tony!" said Mother.

Tony grinned and lifted his hat to them.

Ida looked at his city clothes and asked somberly, "Are you going to Seattle?"

Tony looked hurt. "No, I am not," he said. "I am seeing you off."

As the steamer moved back into the Sound, the launch approached the dock.

Its throbbing motor seemed to draw the people towards it. Ida grabbed at Tony's sleeve. He put his arm around her reassuringly. "It's all right, Daybreak. The first time is the hardest."

Ahead of them, Leroy hugged his family in one all-inclusive embrace and hurried down the dock as though he feared losing his courage.

The Miltons went next—Rose in her mother's arms and Mathew crowding anxiously against his father. At the end of the dock Rose began to cry. Her mother clasped her one more time and handed her into the boat.

"She's only a baby," Annie Ellington murmured behind Ida. "Only a baby."

Ida swallowed. Mother was bending over her, pressing her cheek to Ida's. A tear rolled down Mother's nose and dropped onto Ida's own. She said quickly, "You must not forget how to speak Suquamish with Grandma, Ida. Repeat some words to yourself every day—" She gave Ida a squeeze and let Tony escort her down the dock.

Ida's eyes blurred as Tony kissed her on the forehead and lowered her into the boat. There was no turning back now. She reached for the railing to steady herself.

Next to her, Rose shrank against the side of the boat, sobbing. Ida felt as though the sobs were her own. She tipped up her chin. "It's all right," she said, drawing Rose close. I'm here with you. We'll keep together, Rose."

Behind her she heard Leroy say, "Take hold, Mathew, we're starting to move."

"See you in summer!" Tony called as the quivering launch, its motor growing louder, headed out into the Sound.

Ida looked back to see Mother waving farewell. From the doorway of his house, David Jennings waved, too, as did Katie, standing far up the beach with her little sister on her hip. Above them on the hillside, Little Grandma raised her arm in an arc like the sun's.

Diane Johnston Hamm grew up in western Montana and as a young adult lived in Spain, Mexico, and Colombia. She received a graduate degree in educational psychology from the University of Washington and has been writing for twenty-five years. She is also a self-taught artist.

Among her books for children and young adults are *Bunkhouse Journal*, *Rock-A-Bye-Farm*, and *Laney's Lost Momma*. Mrs. Hamm and her family make their home in Port Townsend, Washington.